Miss
Mamma
Aimee

Books by Erskine Caldwell

For Children:

Anthologies of Erskine Caldwell

by Erskine Caldwell and Margaret Bourke-White

Miss Mamma Aimee

by

Erskine Caldwell

The New American Library

First Printing

Published by The New American Library, Inc.
1301 Avenue of the Americas, New York, New York, 10019

Published simultaneously in Canada
by General Publishing Company, Ltd.

Library of Congress Catalog Card Number: 67-16941

Printed in the United States of America

Miss
Mamma
Aimee

Chapter 1

It was a warm moist morning in the last week of April, with a feel of early summer in the southerly breeze. Cato Boykin, a tall, lanky, balding, and slightly stoop-shouldered fifty-year-old lawyer, got out of his automobile in the circular driveway of the imposing many-roomed Mangrum mansion and went up the jonquil-bordered brick walkway to the veranda.

At that time of day, just a short while before noon, the bright spring sun was almost directly overhead, and Cato walked briskly toward the shade of the portico. The only sound was the monotonous grinding hum of a big yellow bulldozer scraping and terracing the weedy ground on the other side of Mangrum Road, where a large cluster of suburban houses was being built on land that until recently had been part of the Mangrum estate.

As Cato got closer to the house, he could see Martha, Aimee Mangrum's mulatto maid, standing between the white colonnades and watching him, broom in hand. The moment she recognized him she began sweeping the time-worn wooden veranda energetically.

Half an hour earlier, Cato Boykin had received a telephone call from Aimee Mangrum. She had said she wanted to see him right away about a matter of importance. He had been confident that he knew what Aimee wanted to see him about, because she had sent for him many times during the past several years and always for the same purpose.

After talking briefly to her on the phone, Cato had told his secretary to postpone a conference with another attorney until the following week. Then he left his law office on the seventh floor of the Southern Finance Building, got into an elevator after a short wait, and went through a rear door in the lobby to get to his car in the parking lot.

As careful as always, Cato first looked at the tires on his dark-blue four-door sedan to be sure they were in road-worthy condition and then checked the gasoline gauge. After that, driving with care to the end of the narrow alley, he went out Eighth, crossed Broad and Greene, and then, beyond the railroad tracks, took a zigzag course through the sprawling Negro section of the city. Driving slowly through puddles of rainwater all the way from D'Antignac Street to Milledgeville Road, he passed block after block of dilapidated tenements, two-family wooden rentals, weather-grayed shacks, and neighborhood ma-and-pa fish markets and grocery stores.

Each time Cato went in the direction of Mangrum Road, he always traveled the same route through the Negro section instead of taking the faster expressway. This gave him the opportunity to make a passing inspection of the stores and housing owned by some of his wealthy clients. Sometimes a small house or even a two-family dwelling would have been

2

dismantled and every plank of it carried away somewhere overnight to be used to build a squatter shack or to be sold at a junk yard as scrap lumber. He considered it his duty as attorney for his clients to keep a watchful eye on their valuable income-producing property, and when a rental did disappear he would file a theft complaint with the police department and then be able to collect insurance for the owner.

Martha had stopped sweeping when Cato started up the veranda steps and she was waiting for him when he got to the top. He took off his hat and wiped his forehead with the palm of his hand before speaking to her.

"How are you, Martha?"

"I'm pretty well today, Mr. Boykin," she answered hurriedly. "But there's a bad roof leak in that house me and my husband rent on Florence Street. Maybe you could get the man who owns it to fix it."

"I'll see what I can do, Martha. Now, where's Mrs. Mangrum?"

"She's upstairs waiting. Miss Mamma Aimee said she wants you to go right straight upstairs to her room the very minute you get here. She told me to stay out here and tell you that the first thing right away. And just so you'll know about it, Miss Mamma Aimee's acting stiff-necked again. She won't stop to look at anything somebody else wants her to see. Whatever it is she's got on her mind, she's all wrought-up about it."

Nodding understandingly, Cato opened the screen door and went down the dark, wide, high-ceilinged, furniture-cluttered hall to the second-story stairway. It seemed to him that every time he came to the Mangrum house another table or chair or couch had been moved from one of the rooms and crowded into the hall. Aimee had a habit of removing a piece of furniture from a bedroom as a means of getting even with anybody in the house who had displeased her.

3

As Cato started up the long stairway, he saw Aimee waiting for him in the upper hall. As usual, she was wearing one of her droopy, loose-fitting, self-made, floral-print dresses over her hip-heavy fleshy body; and, in a style of her own, her graying brown hair was fluffed and curlicued above her round pink face. She was beckoning excitedly to Cato with jerky motions of her hands.

Aimee was closer to her sixtieth year than to her fiftieth, as Cato, having been her attorney during the ten years since the sudden heart-seizure death of her husband Ralph, knew. But after having passed her forty-ninth birthday she never admitted being another year older, and angrily resented any mention of her possible age. Since Ralph Mangrum's death, and her inheritance of all the family property—which at the time had consisted of the stately Mangrum mansion and nearly eight thousand acres of valuable farm and timber land bordering the southwesterly city limits of Augusta—Aimee had sold large parcels of land from time to time in order to support herself and numerous relatives. As a result, less than a thousand acres of the original plantation now remained.

In addition to Aimee's younger son, Graham, who was thirty years old and unmarried and who had never worked a day in his life, the others who lived on her bounty were her twenty-five-year-old daughter Velma; Velma's guitar-playing husband, Woody Woodruff, who said he was too busy composing and singing folksongs to do any other kind of work; Aimee's brother-in-law, Russell Mangrum; and Russell's constantly complaining wife, Katie.

The twenty-eight-room Mangrum homestead, a grandiose colonial-style mansion that was ample in size to provide lodging for all, had been built by Ralph Mangrum's father early in the century. That was when nearly three dozen Negro families, with many children, worked for cornmeal and fatback and

4

a few dollars a year and produced the Mangrum wealth from the fields and forests of the plantation.

Now, however, not even one Negro family remained. When Graham was twenty years old, he had raped the six-year-old daughter of one of the Negro tenants. To accomplish the rape of this little girl, he had used his pocketknife to slash a larger opening in her body. The girl survived the injury and Graham was not prosecuted, but within a week's time all the Negro families had left the plantation and moved to the Negro district of Augusta. (*That little girl's father was too scared to go to the sheriff or police and a white man could nearly always get away with something like that in those days. But not now. Times have changed too much. If the law didn't get him, somebody would see to it that something bad happened to him.*) Ever since then no Negro tenant farmer could be persuaded to work and live there with his family. Even Martha refused to sleep in a servant's room in the house, but always went back to Florence Street to spend the night with her husband and three daughters.

Because none of the three men in the house—Graham or Russ or Woody—offered to do any work on the remaining acres, the cost of feeding so many people day after day required the frequent sale of parcels of land to provide for everybody. Neither Russ nor Woody had had a steady job since moving into the house, and they had never contributed anything for room and board for their wives or themselves.

In addition, like her son Graham, both Russ and Woody were always hinting to Aimee that they were in need of money to buy gasoline and tires for their rattling old automobiles, as well as five or ten dollars pocket money. Occasionally, the three of them would talk about hiring a white man to farm some of the land with a rented tractor, or getting an engine saw to cut timber for sale, but nothing was ever done about it. As it was, the hilly sand- and clay-uplands of the

5

remaining plantation were covered with an overgrowth of broom sedge and blackjack, while the fertile lowlands and pastures had been abandoned to the wild growth of jimson weed and maypop vines.

Cato Boykin had for many years tried his best to convince Aimee that for her own security and welfare she should stop supporting so many people, because before long there would be no more land to sell and she would be destitute. And in that case, he warned her, she would have to move out of the mansion.

It was at such times that Aimee would wipe tears from her face and say that she felt sorry for her close kin and would be miserable if she could not be kind and helpful to them. Then, after crying for a while, she would become angry and accuse Cato of trying to break up her family and send all her relatives to live in faraway places so she would never see them alive again. It was also at such times that she would accuse Cato of having secretly encouraged her other son, James, who now lived in Atlanta, to go away to college and medical school.

As Cato went up the stairway he hoped that this time Aimee would be in a reasonable state of mind and that their meeting would not end in tears and anger. What he dreaded was being forced to listen to one of Aimee's long tirades blaming him because James had left home and married without her approval, and because Connie, the youngest of her four children, had been away for almost two years without writing even a single letter during that time.

"I'm so glad you got here so soon and are here right now, Cato," Aimee said excitedly when he reached the top of the stairs. She reached out and gripped his arm tensely. "I'm so happy I just had to phone you to hurry out here so I could tell you all about it. I can't think when I've been so happy

6

before, and I couldn't be more sincere if I said it over and over a dozen times."

"That's fine, Aimee," he said cautiously, wondering what she could be talking about. It was unusual for her to be in such good spirits, since ordinarily she was cross and scolded him for not getting there as quickly as she thought he should. He was hopeful that for once she was not going to say she needed money and had to sell some more of the land. "It's good to know you're feeling so fine today. I want to hear all about it. What's the good news, Aimee?"

Still gripping his arm, she took him along the hall toward her room.

"Come on in here with me and make yourself comfortable while I tell you all about it, Cato. I can't hardly believe it myself yet. It's been so long since I've been this happy that I feel like a strange new female all over. It makes me want to exert myself like a love-starved young girl."

Chapter 2

When Aimee and Cato went into the spacious combination bedroom and sitting room, she led him to one of the uphol-stered deep-seated armchairs that had been slipcovered with flowery yellow chintz. It was an enormous room on the south-east corner of the house, even more cluttered with furniture than the downstairs hall. Aimee was continually rearranging the furniture in her own room, just as she liked to do through-out the house, and when Cato came to see her, he always felt he had never been in that room before.

In addition to the four large overstuffed chairs and several smaller ones, there were tall chests of drawers, a fancy dress-ing table, a mahogany writing desk, a foot-treadle sewing machine, a wiry body-form that had been expanded to its limits, and a wide four-poster bed that was so high above the floor that Aimee used a footstool to get into and out of it. The four ceiling-high windows, two facing south and two facing east, were curtained with billowy white drapery.

Aimee seated herself heavily in the chair closest to the one in which Cato sat. After holding her breath tensely for several moments, her heavy breasts rose and fell with a prolonged sigh. Then, her round pink face glowing and her brown eyes blinking, she leaned toward Cato and put her hand on the arm of his chair.

"Now, Aimee, go ahead and tell me what this's all about," Cato said with an encouraging smile.

"Cato, I'm bubbling over so much I can't hardly think what to say first." She sank back into the chair and drew another deep breath. "But the big thing is that the wisdom of fate has given me my true happiness at last."

Cato nodded. "What kind of happiness, Aimee?"

"The happiness of having the true religion for the first time in my life—that's what. And it's so thrilling to talk about it that it makes me feel all light and airy."

"What kind of religion is this, Aimee? You've alway been a faithful, churchgoing Methodist. All the Mangrums have always been good Methodists."

"That's the truth. And God knows like everybody else that I've been a faithful Methodist all my life up to now. But I'm going to withdraw my membership from the Methodists and join up with the true religion. It's been provided by the wisdom of fate and—"

"How did this come about, Aimee? And what is this true religion?"

"Well, I'll tell you all about the whole thing just the way it happened so you'll know about it from the beginning," she said calmly, entwining her chubby fingers and placing her clasped hands on her lap. A placid smile came to her round pink face. "Cato, it all started yesterday afternoon when Martha came up here to my room and said somebody was at the front door wanting to see me about something. What I thought was that it was another of those pesky salesmen trying to sell me something I don't have use for and I told Martha to tell him I didn't want none of whatever it was, but Martha said he didn't have samples of anything showing. When she told me that, I thought it wouldn't do any harm to go down and find out what he wanted to see me about.

"And so, well, when I went down there, there stood the handsomest-looking manly man I'd ever seen in all my life. He looked so handsome that he could've been my own son James himself, and that's who he reminded me of right away—so tall and black-haired and manly and with the kind of eyes that make me feel sorry for a man. I could've mistaken him for James if I hadn't remembered that James stays away and is almost like a stranger to me now.

"But, like I said, that's how handsome he was. My late husband was sort of handsome in an ordinary kind of way, and I truly appreciated Ralph while he was alive, but Ralph was not real tall and solid and bristly-haired, and he never looked like he was standing up erect like a new-set pole in the ground the way I like to see a man do. But don't think I'm finding fault with Ralph. All in all, Ralph was a good man right to the end."

"Yes, Aimee," Cato said, moving to the edge of his chair and waiting to hear what she was going to say next. "I know you were a true and loyal wife to Ralph. Nobody could dispute that. Now what about this man?"

"Well, putting all that about Ralph aside, when I saw this strange man down there at the front door, standing there so tall and handsome with the blackest hair I've ever seen on any man and looking down at me with his great big sorrowful blue eyes—Cato, shivers went all over me from head to

10

foot and I felt hot and cold all at the same time. To tell the honest truth, I'd never felt so sorry for a man before in all my whole life, and I couldn't be more sincere about that. I don't know how long I stood there with the shivers all over me and feeling like I was light-headed and about to float away in the air. And all that whole time all I could think was that I wanted to reach out and touch him and do something for him right then and there. He made me feel so sorry for him—"

"Who was he, Aimee?" Cato asked suspiciously. "What did he want to see you about? Was he selling insurance or something like that? Or did he want to buy some of your land? What was he doing here?"

She shook her head with a serene smile.

"No, Cato. It wasn't anything like that. He wasn't that kind of man. He was a different kind. He told me that he was a mystic preaching-man going around asking people to help him out with a contribution for his church, no matter how little I could spare. He was so manly and talked with so much earnest that the shivers came over me and made me feel so sorry for him—"

"What kind of preacher was he? What church is it?"

"The Supreme Being Missionary."

Cato immediately shook his head. "I never heard of that denomination before, Aimee. And people who go from door to door asking for money—"

"Oh, that's because he just started it himself only three weeks ago when he came to town and rented an old vacant grocery store on Reynolds Street near the levee to preach in. He said when he got converted, God told him to think up a good name for a new church and hurry to Augusta and start preaching. He says he keeps his right ear tuned to God all the time, day and night, because God speaks to him off and on in his right ear and he wouldn't want to miss hearing a single word God says."

"Where did this preacher come from?"

"From up in Tennessee somewhere."

"What's the preacher's name?"

"Pastor Raley Purdy."

She gazed at Cato with a gleaming smile and a misty blinking of her eyes.

"I just can't get over how earnest his name sounds when I say it out loud. Pastor Raley Purdy. Just even to think about his name makes me feel so sorry for him and wanting to do something for him. Pastor Raley Purdy. Pastor Raley Purdy. It brings out the female in me like I'd almost forgot about. Let me hear you say his name, Cato."

Shaking his head, Cato looked down at the threadbare green carpet with a thoughtful frown. During the silence, Aimee lowered her chin and wiped the tears from her cheeks with the back of her hand.

When Cato looked at her again after several moments, he asked, "Did you give him any money, Aimee? You know you can't afford—"

"All I had in my purse was a single dollar bill and a little bit of change and I gave it all to him for his church."

"Well, that's all right, Aimee," Cato told her, relieved to know she had given him no more than that. He leaned back in his chair and nodded approvingly. "I'm glad to hear that's all it amounted to. When you called me up this morning, I was afraid you wanted me to sell some more of your land."

Looking at her with a brief glance, he saw that she was smiling happily to herself.

"And speaking of selling land, Aimee, I want to tell you something. It's a matter I've given a lot of thought to recently. I've decided the wise thing to do now is let me negotiate the best possible sale of every acre you've got left, including this fine old mansion. What I've got in mind is to solicit bids from all the well-financed real estate developers in Augusta who're looking for suburban raw land to subdivide and build new houses on. They're begging for land just outside the city limits, where property taxes are lower, and you couldn't be in a more favorable position."

He paused and glanced at Aimee to see what her reaction was going to be. She said not a word, but he could see that her lips were pressed tightly together and that she was slowly shaking her head.

Looking away from her then, he tried to speak as convincingly and persuasively as possible.

"Aimee, it's not good business to sell off this valuable land piece by piece, acre by acre, or even in parcels of twenty or a hundred acres at a time, and let it continue to dwindle away like it has been doing. Any responsible person would back up that advice. We must think about today's real estate market and take advantage of it. The city is growing out in this direction, the real estate developers are hungry for such desirable land, and I assure you that I can get a fine price from one or more developers for subdividing. Then the money it brings—and I mean a real large amount of cash—can be put in trust for you at one of the banks so you'll have no more worries and a good secure income for the rest of your life."

He was careful not to look at Aimee as he continued.

"Now, about the trust. You can provide in your will that upon your death the trust will be divided equally among your four surviving children. You must consider your and Ralph's children—Velma and Connie and Jim and, especially, Graham. They are entitled to this protection of a trust to keep the whole estate from dwindling to nothing. You could make some provision in the will for your brother-in-law Russell, if you wanted to."

Aimee still had not interrupted him. Encouraged by her silence, Cato began speaking even more forcefully.

"The hard bare fact is that you're supporting too many

13

people now. Without being personal about it, the truth is that every last one of them is taking advantage of you. I tell you, Aimee, the wise thing to do is to get rid of them right away and let them take care of themselves the best they can. Woody Woodruff is as capable of supporting a wife as any other average man, but he's not going to make the slightest effort as long as you let him stay here and live off you. And as for Russ Mangrum—and I don't care if he is your brother-in-law—make him take his wife and get out and earn his own living instead of staying here and being supported like he was a king or something."

He paused, expecting Aimee to say something in protest, but her expression was so placid that he wondered if she had actually heard anything he had said.

"You sent for me this morning, Aimee, now pay attention to me," he told her, raising his voice. "I'm not going to say anything about Graham—he's your son and needs care and that's a personal matter with you. We both recognize the fact that he is somewhat handicapped and has to have special consideration. I'm saying what I did about the others, though, because I consider it my obligation as friend and attorney to protect your interests. I know Ralph would want me to look after you like this. Now, what do you say, Aimee? Are you going to take my advice and authorize me to get out and negotiate the best possible sale of this land for you?"

While he waited to hear what Aimee would say, the only sound to be heard was the grinding hum of the bulldozer scraping and terracing the earth on the other side of the road. Presently, Aimee turned and looked at him, a slowly spreading smile on her round pink face.

"Cato—"

"What is it, Aimee?"

"I sent for you, didn't I?"

He nodded expectantly. "Yes, you did."

14

"Well, the reason I sent for you is because I've made up my mind to deed ten acres of that land at the corner out there so Pastor Raley Purdy can have it to build a fine new church on. And I'll tell you why I made up my mind about it. Late yesterday afternoon I got Graham to drive me downtown to see where Pastor Purdy was preaching at. Well, it was a shabby, run-down, old storefront place on Reynolds Street near the river levee. After I'd looked at it the first time, I told Graham to drive me past it five or six times more, hoping to catch sight of Pastor Purdy, but I never did see him.

"Anyhow, every time I went by that awful place he'd rented for preaching and living in upstairs, I felt so sorry for him that I just had to make up my mind to deed over some of my land so he could build a fine Supreme Being Missionary church where I'll be close to him all the time. I want him to have a fine church built with lasting brick and a real tall white steeple and a shady grove of oak trees all around it. I want him to have a church prettier than anything the Baptists and Methodists have got. Now you know why I sent for you, Cato. I want you to draw up the deed right away for me to sign over to him so he can get started. And I don't want you to be putting off about it, either."

Cato wiped the perspiration from his forehead with a swift motion of his hand.

"You can't do that, Aimee," he protested with a determined shaking of his head. "I won't let you. And I mean what I say. That's final. I'd never be a party to such a foolish thing—it's only a whim of yours, anyway."

She regarded him with a scornful smile.

"Aimee, listen to me. That corner is the most valuable parcel of all the land you've got left. It's an ideal location for a shopping center and it'll bring thousands and thousands of dollars. That money will be a big start to help provide you with a good income as long as you live. That new housing

15

tract that's being developed on the other side of the road—a shopping center and supermarket within a few blocks of hundreds and hundreds of new homes—the population coming in this direction—the scarcity of good commercial real estate—don't think about giving it away for nothing! It makes no sense at all! I won't have a thing to do with it!"

When he paused and glanced at Aimee, he saw that her expression was unchanged and he became even more concerned.

"Aimee, please listen to me," he said, leaning closer to her. "A smart developer would need more than ten acres of such a desirable location. He'd want at least fifty acres—maybe a hundred acres—and he'd have to pay the price we demanded. He would need land for a parking lot for the hundreds of automobiles of the customers who'd be coming to Woolworth's, Grant's, Penney's, the A & P, the E-Z, the I-X-L, the Do-Rite, the coin laundry, liquor store, barber shop, beauty parlor, loan company, pizza bar—"

"Cato, why don't you shut up about that? I told you I want to deed that corner to Pastor Purdy for him to build a fine brick church with a high white steeple."

Cato Boykin stood up and, moving his head discouragedly, took several steps backward toward the door.

"Don't you ever feel sorry for anybody, Cato?"

"No! Not the way you do! Thank God!"

"I'll pity you all your life."

"Save it for yourself."

"I'll be glad to take it back. It'll give me more to feel sorry about for Pastor Purdy. He'll appreciate it."

She sat in rigid silence after that and regarded him with an unblinking stare. Presently, her fleshy chin and neck began to quiver with anger.

"All right, Cato Boykin," she said, raising her voice and sitting up erectly. "I heard what you said. I heard every word of it. Now I'll tell you something. You do like I said or I'll get me

16

another lawyer to do what I want. Nobody's going to keep me from doing what I want to do for Pastor Purdy when I feel sorry for him like I do."

Without a word, Cato moved toward the doorway.

"You go back to your office, Cato Boykin," she called to him in her loud voice, "and when you get there you'd better spend a lot of time thinking about what I said if you know what's good for you. And if you don't tell me sometime tomorrow that you'll draw up the deed like I want it done—well, then it won't do you any good to do no more thinking!"

Neither of them spoke again after that and Cato went down the stairway and through the dark wide hall to the sunlight of the veranda. As he opened the screen door, he heard the casual plunking of a guitar.

Woody Woodruff, seeing Cato come out of the house, fingered the guitar strings several times in a fast tempo. Woody, a slender young man in his mid-twenties, was so short in height that he looked as if he had stopped growing at an early age. (*I sort of like Woody. He may never amount to much making up songs and playing his guitar, but marrying Velma was the best thing that could happen to her. Velma was too pretty and sexy for her own good and she was getting ready to start running wild around town like her sister Connie was doing in those days. It's a pity Connie didn't get married or leave town before she went the way she did.*) When Woody was practicing on the guitar or watching television—even when he was seated at the dining-room table—he had a habit of taking out his comb from time to time and running it through his bushy blond hair and the reddish beard he had been growing for about a year.

As usual at that time of day, after having stayed up most of the night and sleeping all morning, Woody was wearing his favorite pair of tight black pants with his shirttail out and sitting with Velma on the settee at the far end of the veranda

17

while waiting for Martha to ring the dinner bell for the noonday meal. He had kicked off his bright yellow sandals and his bare feet were resting on a chair in front of him.

Cato heard Woody say something to him, but he merely waved his hand in a short gesture and hurried down the steps. When he reached the bottom step and started down the brick walkway toward his car, Woody stood up and called to him in a loud voice.

"Hey, there, Lawyer Boykin!" Woody said. "Wait a minute! Don't try to go slipping off like that! I've got something big-big to find out about!"

Cato stopped and looked back over his shoulder.

"Is Miss Mamma Aimee getting you to sell another piece of land to raise some money?" Woody asked. "You hurry up and do that now, Lawyer Boykin. The sausage around here is getting too fat and greasy to suit me. What I want is some sausage with real lean pork-chop meat in it. And I'm hungry for some big butt ham, too. You picture that, Lawyer Boykin?"

As Cato hurried away without answering, he could hear the sound of the guitar and Woody Woodruff's high-pitched voice singing something about a fat old woman in a big old house who had nothing but hog-belly lard to cook on her kitchen stove.

Chapter 3

Late in the day, after waking up from her afternoon nap, Aimee left her room and called downstairs to Martha.

When Martha finally came out of the kitchen with dragging feet and stood at the bottom of the stairway, Aimee told her to get ready to cook an early supper that night and to be sure to have it on the table by six o'clock sharp.

Martha protested immediately, saying that she had just finished washing the noonday dinner dishes and cleaning up the kitchen, and pleaded that she needed a little more free time in which to sit down and rest her feet for a while before starting another meal.

"Can't you put off eating just a little while longer, Miss Mamma Aimee?" she begged hopefully. "I sure would appreciate that. If I could only have just half an hour to rest up some first—"

"I've got a special good reason for eating supper early tonight," Aimee told her, unmoved by her pleading. "Now, you go ahead and do like I said, Martha. I don't have time to stand here and argue with you about it. I've got to hurry and fix myself up so I'll be ready to go downtown tonight just as soon as I finish my supper. You have a whole day off once in a while to rest up in and you don't have no right to complain like that. Now, stop that fussing and go on and do like I told you at the start. You try my patience with all the complaining you've been doing lately."

She waited impatiently to see that Martha left the downstairs hall and went back to the kitchen. Becoming annoyed when Martha did not go at once, Aimee tried to wave her away with a flinging motion of her arm.

"Well, why don't you do like I told you, Martha?"

Martha leaned wearily on the staircase newel.

"I don't know if I want to keep on working here like the way you make me do for so little pay," she said, looking up at Aimee and ignoring the commanding gestures. "I've been thinking about that a lot lately. It stays on my mind all the time. It's backbreaking to cook all these meals three times every day for all these people in this old house and clean their rooms and pick up after them all the time like I have to do. Looks like they ought to make up their own beds and things like that instead of making me do it for them. If somebody was crippled or bad sick, that'd make a big difference. But now you take that Miss Katie. She sits around all day long and won't never lift a finger to do a single little thing like she ought to with nothing else to do. Yesterday she told me to stoop down and pick up a spool of thread on the floor right beside the chair where she was sitting. She could've

20

reached down and done that. She ought to be ashamed of herself."

"Shut your mouth, Martha Washington!" Aimee yelled down to her. "You know better than to talk like that. You know your place. Don't you dare talk about white people that way. I'm surprised at you saying such a thing."

"I'm only saying what I think, Miss Mamma Aimee," she spoke out boldly. "The old days have gone past and if you don't start paying me more money for all the hard work I'm made to do, I'm apt to pick up and walk out of here some day soon and never—"

"Martha Washington, you listen to me! I'll stop paying you anything at all if you don't shut your mouth and keep quiet. And you've got no business calling me Miss Mamma Aimee, neither. It's not dignified. It sounds like what you'd call somebody running a disreputable rooming house."

"That's what Mr. Woody calls you and it sounds just right to me. It'd be hard for me to get used to calling you anything else now. But I'd have to try to do it if you made me. Anyhow, you couldn't pay me enough to keep quiet about the way I'm treated just because I'm colored."

"I've never heard such back talk to a white woman before in my whole life. But I know what put you up to talking back to me like that. You've been going off to those meetings at night after work and getting your mind all stirred up by your black-race troublemakers. I told you already to stay away from those meetings, didn't I? But I'll warn you just one more time again. And you'd better never let me hear about you getting in with a crowd of your people and marching down the street protesting against white people, and making a big scene at the city hall, neither."

"Reverend Martin Luther King said—"

"Uh-huh! That's exactly what I thought!"

"But Reverend Martin Luther King said people like us—"

"Reverend! Reverend! You talk like he was Reverend Jesus Christ! Jesus Christ was a white man—he wasn't black like that Martin Luther King. You stop talking like he's just as good as Jesus Christ. I won't listen to it."

"Well, all he wants to do is help out the colored the best he can. He knows what a hard life it is for our people the way it is now. He says—"

"You colored people don't have a thing in the world to complain about and stir up trouble. You breathe the air and walk the streets just like white people do. It's the white people who have to struggle and strain to make enough money to pay the colored to work for us."

"But he says if the colored got paid right for the work we do and didn't get cheated at the loan company and didn't have to live in tumbled-down old shacks in mud-puddly alleys and—"

"That's enough of that, Martha Washington!" Aimee said sharply. "Don't get me all wrought-up and on edge with any more talk about that Martin Luther King. I don't have time to argue with you now about a troublemaker like him. If you stop complaining against white people, I'll listen to you some other time!"

Turning away with a hasty smile for Martha, she went toward her room.

"I've got to hurry and fix myself up to go downtown. You do just like I said and everything'll be all right, Martha."

The moment Aimee went into her room and closed the door, Katie came out of her room and walked down the stairs. Katie was a tight-lipped woman in her late forties, with tawny-shaded thin hair and widely-bowed bony legs. As Woody Woodruff said about her when he composed one of his folksongs, when she walked, she looked like somebody carrying a sack of potatoes between her legs and trying to straddle a big puddle of water without getting her feet wet.

22

She had been married to Russ for the past eight years and had lived with him in the same bedroom on the second floor of the Mangrum mansion all that time.

Katie and Russ had no children. On the day they were married, she told Russ that she was not suited by nature for childbirth. He had laughed about it then, thinking the excitement of the wedding had upset her. When they went to bed that night, however, she became hysterical and hit the top of his plunger such a hard blow with her hairbrush that it dripped blood on the sheet.

After that first night, Katie put a heavy iron curtain-rod in the middle of the bed between the sheets, and she had kept it there ever since. When Russ complained about it, she told him that it would have to stay there to keep him from getting close enough to breathe on the back of her neck while she was asleep and make her catch pneumonia. Russ soon became acquainted with a divorced waitress in one of the downtown cafés who lived alone in a small gray bungalow on Telfair Street and who had been friendly and accommodating ever since. As for Katie, she sewed and knitted and rarely left the house except when she made Russ take her to a funeral and to the Church of Christ on Sunday mornings.

Without speaking to Katie, Martha left the hall and went to the kitchen to cook supper. She had been there for only a few minutes when Katie opened the door and then closed it noisily behind her.

"Somebody took my sewing table out of my room today," Katie stated accusingly. "Where is it?"

"Don't look at me when you say that, Miss Katie," Martha told her, slamming an iron skillet on the stove. "I don't get paid much for cooking and nothing at all for taking blame. You'll have to find somebody else to fuss at about that."

"Well, it's gone out of my room, anyhow."

"I believe you. And you've lived in this house just as long

23

as I've been working here and you ought to know by now who's always picking up a piece of furniture one place and putting it down somewhere else when she's peeved and stiff-necked about something."

"Well, have you seen my table anywhere, Martha?"

"No, ma'm, I sure haven't."

"Where would she take it to and hide it?"

"I don't know that, either, Miss Katie. I can't be looking after every piece of furniture in this big old house with all the other work I'm made to do. That sewing table's liable to be 'most anywhere in all these rooms."

"Well, if you come across it anywhere, let me know. I need it real bad to lay out a pattern on for a new dress I'm ready to make. You won't see me getting down on my knees on the floor for that."

"I reckon not, Miss Katie," Martha remarked vaguely, with a sympathetic motion of her head. "It's a real shame about that. I know just exactly how you feel."

Katie came closer to the stove then and stood beside Martha. She watched in silence while Martha greased the big iron skillet.

"Supper's going to be a whole hour early tonight," Martha said as she spread the grease on the hot skillet. "Miss Mamma Aimee said to have it ready and on the table at six o'clock sharp and it's getting close to that time already. I told her I needed some rest first, but she wouldn't listen to me. I don't know what her main hurry's about, but she acts like she's got something big on her mind. You never know about her when she takes a notion and gets stiff-necked about something or other."

"I don't know why she's hurrying up supper tonight, either," Katie said immediately, "but I know something else."

"You do?" Martha asked interestedly, looking up from the stove. "What is it you know, Miss Katie?"

24

Katie glanced behind her to see if anybody had come into the room while her back was turned.

"Somebody's going to get even with her one of these days for all her meanness. Somebody's going to pay her back for the way she treats people. Taking away furniture from somebody she's mad at and hiding it away in her room or somewhere else in the house—it's the downright meanness of a mean woman. That's what it is. Pure meanness. She's always putting on a sad face and saying she feels so sorry for people and then turning right around and treating me and everybody else in the house like common dirt. There's hardly a stick of furniture left in my room now, except some old rickety chairs and the bed. You just wait and see. Somebody's going to get even with her one of these days and pay her back good and plenty."

"What would somebody start out to do to get even with her, Miss Katie?"

"I'm not saying. There're a lot of ways. But just one of the ways would be enough to pay her back for all her meanness. And I'm just waiting and counting the days for it to happen to her, too."

Martha looked at her closely for a moment. "You don't mean something real bad, do you, Miss Katie?"

"I don't mean something only halfway bad. That wouldn't be good enough to get even with her all the way."

"Well," Martha said, "I reckon anybody could move out of this house and live somewhere else if they didn't like it here enough to stay and put up with Miss Mamma Aimee. Miss Connie and Mr. James did that a long time ago. It looks to me like too many kinfolk people still live cooped up together in this house. They're always quarreling and pecking on each other about some little something or other. I've never seen a house big enough for so many kinfolk people to live in and not quarrel all the time."

25

"I'm not moving an inch," Katie stated with a tightening of her lips. "I married to have a home and I'm going to live here as long as I please. I wouldn't have got married in the first place if it wasn't for that. But it wouldn't bother me a bit if some of the others moved out and stayed away, though. I don't like to mention real names, but you know who I'm talking about. That good-for-nothing Woody Woodruff and that half-minded Graham—"

"Maybe it's all right for you to talk like that, Miss Katie, but it's not my place to listen to it."

Katie turned and walked out of the kitchen, slamming the door behind her.

Glancing at the clock on the shelf above the stove, Martha hurriedly set the dining-room table and then carried the serving dishes in from the kitchen. After everything had been done, she went to the hall and rang the big brass supper bell for everybody to come to the table.

Chapter 4

Wearing a newly made floral-print dress and a matching small summer hat, and with a bright reddish tint spread unevenly on her cheeks, Aimee was the first to come into the dining room. She seated herself in her chair at the head of the table and was helping herself from the serving dishes when the others came into the room one by one and sat down at their usual places.

Puffy-cheeked and sullen, moving as if guiding his bulging belly toward his place at the foot of the table, Graham was the last to get there. As soon as he sat down, Aimee bowed her head and mumbled a few words of grace. Then, as customary, leaning forward and pointing at Graham, she passed the serving dishes to him so he could have generous portions before the others took too much of the food.

"Help yourself to all you want, Graham," his mother told him. "There's always plenty for you."

Russ and Katie sat together on one side of the long table, and Woody and Velma were on the other side. While waiting for Graham to help himself to all he wanted, Woody took out his comb and ran it slowly through his long blond hair and scraggly red beard. When he had finished and put the comb back into his shirt pocket, Velma cuddled against him and, giggling a little, fondly stroked his reddish beard with her fingers.

Russ, with a faint smile, leaned back in his chair and fixed his gaze upon Woody's untrimmed beard.

"How many weeks has that bunch of jimson weeds been growing on your face?" he said to Woody.

"I haven't added up lately."

"When are you going to chop it off?"

"That's my business and wouldn't you like to know."

"It looks to me like the only business you ever work at."

"It's more than anything you work at."

"If I had me a razor sharp enough," Russ said, "I'd go to work and scrape it off your face right now."

"If you don't know how to strop a razor, why don't you go to a barber college and learn how?"

"I might do that. Then I could let it accidentally slip down your face to where it would do more good."

There was an interval of silence in the room while they glared across the table as if daring each other to say another word.

"I think Woody has a wonderful beard," Velma spoke up, putting her hands on both sides of Woody's face. "It's so distinguished-looking—so manly." She ran her fingers through the reddish hair. "It gives me such a thrilling sensation just to feel it. Haven't you ever felt the same way when you touched something like that with your hands, Uncle Russ?"

28

He nodded. "It makes me shudder, too—just like getting too close to a mangy dog."

"Will you please say that again so I can get a good picture of what I'm beating hell out of you for?" Woody said to Russ. "I want to double-check the focus."

"You don't have enough muscle to bait a fishhook."

Woody rolled up his sleeve. "You want to feel my muscle before I knock hell out of you so when you wake up you'll know what hit you?"

Aimee rapped her plate with her knife.

"Now, I want everybody to act nice and friendly at the table," she said with a quick smile. "This is no place for harsh words. It's the only time we all get together in a home-folks way and I want it to be calm and pleasant."

Reaching for the dish of potatoes in front of Graham, Russ helped himself to several large scoops with the spoon and then passed the dish to Katie. When all the serving dishes were finally shoved across the table to Woody and Velma, they shared what was left of the fried potatoes, sausage cakes, and hot biscuits.

After placing the one remaining pan-size sausage cake on his plate and looking at the globs of hog fat oozing from it, Woody squeezed it against the plate with the heel of his hand until he could get no more grease out of it. Then tilting his plate, he poured and scraped several spoonfuls of the white lardlike grease into one of the empty dishes. After that, he put his arms on the table, lowered his head over the plate, and hurriedly ate every morsel of it.

While Graham was pouring a generous amount of molasses over his biscuits, Woody pushed back his chair and reached for his guitar. After some preliminary strumming and tuning of the strings, and gazing at a crack in the ceiling, he began to compose one of his folksongs. This time, plucking the guitar in a slow tempo, he began singing a lament in his high-pitched voice about a grown-up man who was a mamma's boy all his life and never had a girl for a kissing date.

Woody had started another verse when Graham, without saying a word, suddenly drew back his arm and slammed his fist against the side of Woody's head. (*I wouldn't want to be around Graham Mangrum very much. It's too dangerous. I've never seen anybody lose his temper as quick as he does. His mother is the only one who can calm him down when he gets mad, but sometimes she acts like she's not even trying to do that. And don't think she won't get mad in a hurry, too.*) Woody fell backward out of his chair, the guitar striking the dining-room wall with a resounding musical thud, and he was still on the floor when Graham got up and tried to stomp Woody's head. Before he could do this, though, Velma got in front of her brother and then Russ shoved him away.

"That's enough of that, Graham," Aimee spoke to him calmly, at the same time lightly rapping her knife on the table. "Now, you quit what you're doing. That's no way to behave in the dining room at mealtime. It's not nice and I won't like you if you do things like that. You want me to like you, don't you, Graham?"

"Then tell him to quit making fun of me like that all the time," Graham said, backing away obediently.

"He didn't mean any harm, Graham," Velma told her brother as she helped Woody from the floor. "He can't keep from making up folksongs about anything he happens to think of. He's like that all the time. Woody's just made that way."

"I don't care how he's made," Graham said, his face still flushed with anger. "You'd better make him quit singing songs about me. And if he don't stop making fun of me like that, I'll jump on him and stomp his face so he'll look like he was made some other way. I don't like him."

Graham took out his pocketknife and opened the blade.

"I don't want him married to Velma."

30

"Put that away, Graham," Aimee told him. "I won't like you if you don't."

He closed the blade and put the knife into his pocket.

Aimee got up from the table and carefully smoothed the wrinkles from her skirt.

"Now I want to know something," she said, smiling pleasantly. "I want to know who's going to drive me downtown right away. I want to leave the house in no more than ten minutes from now so I'll be there by seven-thirty sharp without fail. Who's going to take me?"

"Are you going to a movie tonight, Mamma?" Velma asked.

"Certainly not," she said at once. "I wasn't thinking of such a thing. I'm going to Wednesday-night prayer meeting at Pastor Raley Purdy's church on Reynolds Street. And I want to be there the whole time he's preaching and praying and not miss a single word of what he says. Now, who's going to drive me downtown right away?"

There was silence in the room until she spoke again.

"I want somebody to take me for the sake of my new religion," she said urgently. "Everybody knows I can't drive a car myself. I never learned how."

"Well, I'm going bowling with my team tonight, Aimee," Russ said when she looked at him. "I just couldn't spare the time going somewhere else first."

Woody was already shaking his head when Aimee turned and looked at him.

"Not me, Miss Mamma Aimee," he told her emphatically. "I'm working out tonight with my combo way-to-hell-and-gone on the other side of town. I picture a job coming out of that and I couldn't skip it."

Aimee went to the doorway where Graham was standing.

"Mamma, there's not enough gas in our car to get there and back," he told her. "The gas tank's just about bone-dry."

"Never mind about that, Graham." She patted his arm.

"We'll stop at a filling station and I'll cash a check. I need a little money to put in the church collection basket, anyway. Now hurry up and let's go, Graham."

Aimee went up to her room for a final look at herself in the mirror to see if she needed more powder on her face and neck.

When she came down to the veranda after a few minutes, the sun was still shining on the highest branches of the oak trees, but the heat of the day had passed and the evening breeze from the coast was coming up the river valley and gently rustling the mimosas. The big yellow bulldozer that had been grinding monotonously hour after hour all day long now stood silently on the newly scraped earth across the road. The only sounds were the pleasant chirpings of the twilight birds in the mimosa trees and the rhythmic croaking of the frogs on the reedy banks of Mangrum Pond behind the house.

Neither Woody nor Russ had left the house yet and Graham was waiting for his mother in the dusty old car at the end of the brick walkway. Aimee stopped only long enough along the way to pick some yellow jonquils for a small bouquet to take to Raley Purdy.

It was a quarter of a mile to the nearest filling station, which was at the junction of Mangrum Road and the southside expressway, and they got to it before all the gasoline in the tank had been used.

Aimee told Bunson, the Negro boy who worked at the filling station, to pump two dollars' worth of gasoline into the tank. While Bunson was doing that, she opened her purse and wrote a check for three dollars. When she handed the check to Bunson, she told him to hurry and bring back a dollar in small change of nickels, dimes, and quarters.

There was such a long delay that Aimee became impatient, and she reached over and blew the horn several angry blasts. Finally, instead of Bunson bringing her the dollar in change,

32

Gene Infinger, the owner of the filling station, came walking slowly from his office. Gene was a tall, big-muscled man with a wide sun-browned face and thick black eyebrows. As always, he was wearing open-necked, grease-stained, tan coveralls.

"Where's my dollar change?" Aimee demanded in a loud voice. "I'm in the biggest kind of hurry to get downtown. I told that nigger boy to hurry up and bring me my money. Looks like you'd make him do like he ought to for white people who stop here to buy your gasoline."

Gene said nothing to Aimee until he had reached the side of the car.

"Mrs. Mangrum," he said solemnly, holding up a bank check in each hand for her to see, "it'd be a good thing for you to slow down the way you talk."

"I'm in a big hurry, Mr. Infinger. Give me my money."

"Mrs. Mangrum, a few days ago you gave me a check for two dollars' worth of gas and today it bounced back from the bank. I want your business if you'll pay cash, but I won't sell you another drop of gas if you're going to try to pay for it with one of your checks when you don't have enough money in the bank to make good on it. Now, you hand me the four dollars you owe me in cash, and I'll tear up both of these checks and you can be on your way. All you have to do is that, and I won't make a bit of trouble for you."

"Please don't stand there and hold me up any longer talking like that, Mr. Infinger," she pleaded frantically. "I'm in the biggest kind of hurry now. I'll take care of everything in a few days. I couldn't be more in earnest when I say that. Please give me my change in nickels, dimes, and quarters. I need the money for the church collection at prayer meeting tonight and I don't want to be late getting there. Don't do me like this. I've got to have the money. I'd be ashamed of myself

33

to go there and let people see me not put money in when they pass the collection basket."

She held out her hand, but Gene shook his head and took a step backward.

"You're not going to take my money and put it in some church collection like you're talking about. If I wanted to do that, I'd put it in myself."

"This is a terrible way to drive up to a filling station and be treated. I'm Mrs. Mangrum—and you know it. Everybody knows me."

"It wasn't me who started this trouble, Mrs. Mangrum. And you can't talk me out of my money no matter who you are or what you say. You've been giving me no-good checks to pay for gas for a long time now. I've had to wait a month or more sometimes for you to make good on them and now I'm fed up with it. To make it worse, this time you're trying to give me another worthless check for gas and even want a dollar in cash besides. I'm not that big a fool."

"You're just not one of the good people, Mr. Infinger. You don't act like somebody born and raised here like the rest of us. I've been suspicious of a name like yours."

Putting the two checks into his pocket, Gene called Bunson and told him to get a hose and drain out the exact amount of gasoline he had pumped into the tank.

"I've never been insulted like this before in my life!" Aimee said loudly. "You're no gentleman, Mr. Infinger!"

"And you're not so ladylike yourself—coming here to get gas with a bum check and then getting mad because I won't give you a dollar in cash besides."

When Aimee saw Bunson coming to the car with a bucket and hose, she pushed Graham with both hands.

"Graham! Don't let that nigger boy take the gasoline out of the tank! Do something! Get out there and stop him! Don't let a nigger do such a thing!"

34

Graham opened the door and went to the rear of the car. While he was shoving Bunson away from the tank, Gene Infinger reached behind the steering wheel and took the ignition key from the lock. Putting the key into his pocket, Gene walked toward Graham.

"Leave that boy alone, Graham," he ordered.

"She told me to make him stop."

Graham shoved Bunson again.

"I don't care what she said," Gene told him, "but you'd better listen to what I say. Don't put your hand on Bunson again or I'll beat hell out of you. And nobody's coming here and going away with my gas without paying for it. I used to think a lot of your daddy while he was alive, but I don't have no use for nobody with the Mangrum name now."

Carefully watching Graham's feet in case Graham tried to kick him, Bunson got down on his knees and unscrewed the top on the gasoline tank.

"I've been losing gas at night after I close up and go home," Gene was saying, "and I've got a damn good idea where it's going. Somebody's picking the lock on my storage tank and using a suction pump on it to get gas out. You'd better keep the hell away from my filling station from now on even if you've got money. One of these nights I'm going to stay up and blast the guts out of somebody with my shotgun, and I won't give a damn who it is, neither. If it's you, I'll be glad it wasn't somebody else."

Graham took his knife from his pocket, but Gene kicked it out of his hand before he could open the blade. Angered, he jumped at Gene, swinging his fists, but Gene quickly stepped aside. When Graham lunged at him a second time, the fight was over as soon as Gene hit him a stunning blow on the face and knocked him to the ground.

Bunson finished draining the exact amount of gasoline into a bucket and carried it to the shed while Graham was getting to his feet and dazedly rubbing his face. While he stood there, Gene threw the car keys and knife at him and walked away.

Aimee was crying and moaning when Graham started the engine of the car and drove from the filling station.

"It's too late to go to the prayer meeting now even if we went to another filling station and tried to get some gasoline," she wailed. "It's so late now I'd miss hearing half of what Pastor Purdy was preaching about. And I don't have the money to put in the collection, anyhow. Take me home, Graham."

While Graham was driving slowly down Mangrum Road in the early darkness, hoping there was enough gasoline left in the tank to take them all the way home so he would not have to get out and walk, his mother was wiping tears from her face with both hands and sobbing brokenly.

"I feel so sorry for myself . . . I can't get downtown to see Pastor Purdy . . . Pastor Purdy would comfort me . . . I want to be where he is . . . I need him all the time now . . . He'd comfort me every minute . . . I feel so sorry for myself . . ."

Just before they entered the driveway, Aimee leaned out the window as far as she could and hurled the bouquet of jonquils into the watery drain ditch with all her might.

Chapter **5**

Aimee was up and dressed much earlier than usual the next morning even though she had tossed and turned and gotten very little sleep during the night. The embarrassment of not having enough money to buy gasoline for her car at the filling station, and her fervent desire to do something for Raley Purdy, had kept her awake almost until dawn.

On her way downstairs for breakfast, Aimee rapped loudly on the door of Russ's room until she finally woke him up, and then she told him that she wanted him to hurry and get ready to drive her downtown so she could attend to an important matter.

Russ grumbled and complained about being made to get up so early in the morning after not having gotten home from

37

bowling until midnight, and it was nearly half an hour before he came stomping down the stairs and into the dining room. He still had not shaved that morning, and the black stubble on his face made him look more disgruntled and ill-humored than usual.

"Why can't you wake up Graham and make him take you?" Russ said gruffly as he sat down at the table. "He's got nothing else to do. Why can't he do something? Woody Woodruff never does nothing, neither. Why do you pick on me and make me do it?"

Ignoring Russ as if she had not heard him speak at all, Aimee told Martha to hurry and not waste a minute serving him breakfast. Before going to the kitchen, Martha muttered something about being in a bigger hurry to get more pay for all the work she had to do.

"You know when I stay up late bowling I need my sleep in the morning," Russ continued to complain, scowling at Aimee across the table. He rubbed his eyes and the stubble on his face with both hands. "You didn't even give me time to shave. Why can't you make Graham get out of bed and take you downtown in your own car? You always make me do what he ought to do. It just ain't fair to make me get up this early and let him stay in bed."

"I've got my own good reason for not going in my car and I'm not going to waste time talking about it. Now, you hurry up and eat your breakfast and let's go. I've got to see Cato Boykin as fast as I can about something of big importance before he goes ahead and does something that I've changed my mind about."

"If you're in such a big hurry why can't you phone the lawyer, instead of making me take you to see him?"

"Because. Nobody could transact the kind of business that I'm talking about on the phone and get it done the way I want it. And besides, Graham said there's not enough gasoline in my car to get downtown."

"All you'd have to do is stop at Gene Infinger's filling station and buy some."

"I don't want to hear another word about that," she said sharply, rapping her knife on the table. "I'll never buy another drop of gasoline from that Gene Infinger as long as I live. I want everybody in this house to stop buying gasoline from him, too."

"What happened at Gene Infinger's that made you mad?"

"He insulted me—treating me like I was a nobody."

"What did he say to insult you?"

"It's too disgusting to talk about. Now you hurry up like I told you, Russell. I'm going out there now and wait for you in your car."

After leaving the dining room and getting into Russ's fender-dented green sedan in the driveway, Aimee waited only a few minutes before she impatiently began blowing the horn. When Russ finally came out of the house and got into the car, he slammed the door so hard the clattering rattle echoed from the side of the house. Racing the noisy engine, he started off with a violent jerk that hurled Aimee's head backward and left a throbbing pain in her neck.

Not a word was said as they went up Mangrum Road. Aimee was sitting as far away from Russ as she could, staring straight ahead with both hands clutching her neck as they passed Gene Infinger's filling station. After that, they continued to ride in silence all the way along the expressway until they reached Broad Street and turned into the parking lot behind the Southern Finance Building.

"Well, what do you expect me to do now?" Russ asked gruffly when she got out of the car to go up to Cato Boykin's office. "I don't want to waste time staying here. I want to go home and sleep some."

"You wait right here," she ordered as she walked away. "Don't you dare drive off and leave me behind."

It was only a few minutes after eight o'clock when Aimee entered Cato's office on the seventh floor of the building. She walked through the reception room and opened the door to his private office without knocking.

As had been his custom for many years, Cato was usually in his office by eight o'clock in the morning, although his secretary did not arrive until nine. When asked why he came so early, he would say that he was able to get his best work of the day done without distractions before the phone began ringing.

Cato looked up with an annoyed frown when the door opened and he saw Aimee. (*"I like my profession and I wouldn't be happy doing anything else, but I often wish I could eliminate two types of cases that are almost always disagreeable. The most unpleasant of all are divorces and financial settlements. The other type of case is trying to protect, and not always successfully, an elderly widow with considerable property and keep her from giving it all away to begging outsiders and opportunists instead of conserving it for rightful heirs or for worthy educational and charitable organizations."*) He slowly got to his feet as she crossed the room.

"I've changed my mind," Aimee announced as she sat down in the chair beside his desk. "That's why I got up so early this morning to come to tell you."

"Well, that's fine, Aimee," he said, too surprised by her statement to be annoyed any longer. He sat down again. "Just what did you change your mind about?"

"Cato, I want you to go ahead the way you talked about doing yesterday and sell off everything at once this time. That's what I changed my mind about and it was the wisdom of fate that did it. I stayed awake nearly all night long worrying myself sick about it and then all at once the wisdom of

40

fate told me what to do. Now, don't you go thinking up something different. I need the money worse than ever before and I want it right away."

Cato leaned back in his chair, nodding his head slowly as he looked at her and wondering what had been the cause of her change of mind.

"Do you know that last night Gene Infinger wouldn't sell me two dollars' worth of gasoline for my car and give me a dollar in change when I wrote out a check for three dollars?"

"No, I didn't know about that, Aimee," he said, shaking his head with concern.

"And then when he wouldn't sell me the gasoline and give me the money, he picked a fight with Graham and knocked him down on the ground. He treated me and Graham like the same kind of nobody he is himself."

"Aimee, I'm sorry to hear this—especially about Graham being in another fight."

"It wasn't Graham's fault. He was trying to keep that nigger boy who works there from taking the gasoline out of my car."

"I don't know about that, but I do know you don't have a single dollar in the bank to buy gasoline or anything else. The bank phoned me late yesterday afternoon and told me so. And I knew I'd be hearing from you very soon when the bank said some of your checks had been refused payment for lack of sufficient funds in your account. I didn't call you then because I didn't want you to be distressed and have to endure a long night of worry about it. I'd planned to phone you later this morning. Now I'm glad I waited and that you came here instead to talk about such a serious matter."

Aimee smiled meekly. "Well, I was ashamed to mention it a minute ago, but that was the whole cause of all the trouble at the filling station last night when I wanted to buy some gasoline with another check."

"I'm sorry you were embarrassed like that," he told her sympathetically. "Such things are very disagreeable."

"Well, you go ahead now and do the way you said yesterday about selling all my property and getting all the money for me at one time. And I want it right away, too. I need it to buy some gasoline for my car and buy food for the household and pay Martha Washington what I owe her to keep her quiet and for a lot of other things, too. My shoes are so shabby I'm ashamed to be seen on the street wearing them. How soon can I get the money?"

"Now just a minute, Aimee," he spoke patiently. "You're leaping ahead too fast. It can't be done with a snap of the fingers. It may take a week, a month, or even longer, and I won't handle it any other way. Disposing of the kind of real estate you own is a serious matter and I'm going to be careful and deliberate about it for your sake. You have almost a thousand acres of valuable property left now and I'm not going to let you dump it on the market for a penny less than its full value."

"How much money is that?"

"I don't know yet. First of all we'll have an appraisal made. Then we'll ask for bids and go on from there. However, I can tell you this about it. Something can be done in the meantime to take care of your essential needs. I'll arrange for a short-term loan, putting up your property as security, and then the note can be paid off as soon as the sale has been completed and the proceeds are in hand."

Aimee nodded agreeably for a brief moment. She started to say something, but Cato held up his hand to stop her.

"And then the next step," he continued, "will be to use the remaining proceeds—and I'm confident there will be a considerable amount of those—anyway, the remaining proceeds will be used to establish a trust with income payable to you during your lifetime and providing for the corpus to be dis-

42

tributed equally among your four children. Ralph instructed me to draw up a new will for him with those precise provisions, but he did not live to sign it—his sudden death—"

"No!" Aimee said emphatically. "It's all my own property now and I'm going to do with it as I please. And if you won't do like I want—"

"All right, Aimee," he said resignedly, realizing it was useless to try to reason with her in her present state of mind. "Perhaps it'll be best to talk it over some other time. Now, let's see. How much ready cash do you think you need right away?"

"All I can get."

"Now, Aimee, please be reasonable. Don't take that attitude. Every dollar borrowed on the note has to be repaid and it's not money to be squandered. Let's be realistic about it. Let's estimate your essential needs for, say, the next three months. What would you figure your necessary household and personal expenses to be for that length of time? Five hundred dollars? Seven-hundred-fifty?"

Closing her lips tightly, she remained silent.

"A thousand dollars, Aimee?"

She nodded with a pleased smile.

"That's a lot of money. But all right. I'll advance you a hundred out of pocket right now and have the remaining nine hundred for you as soon as the papers can be drawn for your signature."

Aimee leaned over the desk and watched as he began counting out the hundred dollars in five- and ten-dollar bills that were limp and soiled with use. He paused after counting only a part of the money.

"I'm very pleased that you made this sensible decision, Aimee. I'd hate to see you sell off a few more acres to get a thousand dollars and then in two or three months have neither land nor money left. I admire your shrewd judgment."

43

She motioned with her hand for him to continue taking the money from his wallet.

"I'm going to take that awful money home and wash and iron it so it'll be fit to handle. If there's one thing I can't stand, it's ragged dirty old money."

"It's all right for you to wash and iron it, Aimee, but there's something else I want you to do." He slowly counted out a few more bills. "No matter what condition the money is in, clean or dirty, it's for you to use only for your essential personal and household needs. Don't give a single dollar of it away no matter how sorry you are for somebody."

Aimee nodded impatiently after listening to his advice, but Cato still did not finish counting out the money he was going to give her.

"Aimee, sometimes you remind me of a nice old lady who walks around town looking in alleys for stray cats and ends up feeding a hundred of them in her house and then has to go hungry herself."

"All I've got is just one old tomcat to my name and all I feed Sonny Boy is scraps from the table," she protested.

"I know, but just look at all the people in your house you're feeding much more than you would a hundred stray cats."

"I feel sorry for them."

"And I feel sorry for you, too."

"I didn't ask you for your sympathy."

"It'll always be available whenever you need it."

He handed Aimee the money and she quickly stuffed it into her purse. Looking at him severely for a moment after that, she got up from the chair and went toward the door.

"You tend to your business, Cato Boykin, and I'll tend to mine," she called to him as she was leaving the office. "The Mangrums don't need your pity. We've got our family pride."

Cato followed her down the corridor to the elevator.

"Now, Aimee, there's just one more thing," he said with

44

concern as she waited for the elevator. "It's about that evangelist who came to your house yesterday. I hope you realize that you can't deed any part of your land to him for a church. It's been agreed between us that we're going to offer your property for sale as a whole and without exceptions. That is your understanding, isn't it?"

"I changed my mind about doing that, Cato," she told him, smiling pleasantly. "Building a church would take too long. I decided to do something else right away for Pastor Purdy instead. It'll be better for him now and lots quicker."

"What, Aimee? What are you talking about? You don't mean you're going to give him some of that hundred dollars— or all of it—do you? Because if you do, I won't make any move at all to arrange that loan. I'm putting my foot down about that."

"Don't you worry, Cato," she said with her pleasant smile as she patted his arm. "It's not going to be anything like that. What I'm doing is inviting Pastor Purdy to come live with me in my house so I can take care of him. I feel so sorry for him living all alone and trying to cook his own meals and things like that he told me about. I couldn't get any peaceful sleep last night, just thinking about it. If I dozed off, I'd wake up crying because I felt so sorry for him. Then by the time daylight came, the wisdom of fate told me what to do. It's a shame for a fine man like him trying to get along without a woman's care for his comfort. He needs a woman to do little personal things for him that only a woman knows how. I'll help him get some land for a new church some other time. That can wait a while now. The first thing I'm going to do for him is take care of him in a womanly way."

"Does he know about this yet—this invitation to live with you?"

"No, not yet. But he soon will. I'm on my way right now to

surprise him about it. Don't you want to go with me and see how pleased he'll be when I tell him?"

"No, I do not."

"Then I'll tell you all about it afterward."

"And he won't be paying you for room and board?"

"Of course he won't. I'm giving him pure hospitality."

"You're giving yourself the cost of feeding another—"

The door of the elevator opened and Aimee stepped inside before anything more could be said. With a bright smile on her round pink face, she waved gaily to him as the door slowly closed between them.

When Aimee got to the parking lot, Russ was asleep on the front seat of his faded green sedan with his mouth open and one leg dangling over the side of the door. She had to shake him roughly several times before he opened his eyes. When he finally moved and pushed himself upright on the seat, he gazed dazedly at Aimee's face as though he had never seen her before, and then he looked all around the parking lot as if wondering where he was.

Russ was still sleepy-eyed when he turned and looked at Aimee a second time as she got into the car and sat down on the seat beside him. Still not speaking to him, Aimee urged him to start the engine by impatiently motioning with her hand.

Russ yawned. "I don't know how long you stayed away," he said in a mumbling voice, "but it wasn't long enough for me to get much of my sleep back. I'm going home now and catch up with the rest of it."

"No, you don't," she told him. "I'm not ready to go home yet. I want you to drive me over to the Supreme Being Missionary church on Reynolds Street. And quit that complaining and wasting time. Start up this car. I'm in a big hurry to get there."

"Why do I have to go over there?" he grumbled. "They

don't have preaching going on at this time of day. And it ain't even Sunday, neither."

"Never mind about that, Russell. You just go ahead and do like I say. I've got my own good reason for it. I'm going to pay a personal call on Pastor Purdy about something important that can't wait. Now, you start up this car and drive me over there like I'm telling you."

"You're getting as bossy as Katie is."

"Don't you compare me with her. I won't stand for it."

After again racing the engine noisily and putting the car into gear with a jerk that tossed Aimee's head backward, Russ drove from the parking lot and went slowly along Reynolds Street to the storefront church.

The ground floor of the sagging two-story wooden building looked as deserted as all the other window-boarded stores along the street and as far back as the levee, but on the second floor a single window was open and the strident sound of gospel singing could be heard on a radio. Aimee told Russ to stop the car in front of the building and to wait for her until she came back.

"I want to go home," he said. "I don't want to waste any more time waiting around here like this."

"You're going to wait for me right here like I tell you."

Leaving Russ slumped glumly in the car, and warning him again not to drive away without her, Aimee cautiously climbed the loose-boarded steps on the outside of the building to the narrow landing at the top. As soon as she could get her breath back, she knocked on the door several times.

When there was no answer to her knocking, she began pounding on the flimsy door with her fist. That was when the radio suddenly became silent. A moment later the door was opened and Raley stood there, barefooted and dressed only in baggy tan pants and a dingy-looking undershirt.

Open-mouthed with surprise, he was staring at Aimee.

"Oh, my God!" she cried out. "You're not Pastor Purdy! Who're you? Where am I?"

She backed away from the door and started toward the steps.

"Yes, I'm him, Mrs. Mangrum," he was quick to tell her then. "This is me. Pastor Purdy."

She shook her head with a doubtful expression. "But you don't look like yourself. Your face looks a lot like I remember it, but the rest of you don't. Yesterday you had on a fine-looking black suit and a yellow-dotted necktie and your hair was combed and parted so nice."

"That suit of clothes you saw me in was what I wear when I'm doing my religious work, Mrs. Mangrum," he explained earnestly. "The rest of the time like now I save it and wear my old clothes like this. I wasn't doing any religious work this morning except listening to gospel singing on the radio and so I put these clothes on."

"I feel so sorry for you, Pastor Purdy," Aimee told him with a drooping of her mouth as she looked at his soiled under-shirt. "I want to wash your clothes for you."

As he looked down at his undershirt and bare feet, a flush came to his pallid face. Suddenly turning away without a word, he went back into the room and hastily put on a rum-pled white shirt that had been hanging on the back of the chair. After partly tucking his shirttail into his pants, he put on his shoes without waiting to find his socks.

Chapter 6

While Raley put on his shirt and shoes, Aimee, looking into the room from where she stood on the narrow porch, could see a paint-chipped, iron-frame bed with a bare mattress and a soiled gray-tick pillow. Near the bed was Raley's small radio on a wooden crate, a large pearl-handled revolver and a thick Bible on the table, and a single chair. The window had neither a curtain nor a shade over it, there was no rug on the plank floor, and the ceiling was rain-stained and sagging in two of the corners. On a shelf above the cold-water basin was a rusty hot-plate, and on the floor under the basin was a dented tin pan and a chipped china plate and a discolored coffee cup. Raley's black suit was hanging on a nail in the wall.

Wiping tears from her eyes, Aimee moved backward against the porch railing and would not let herself look at the dismal room again.

When Raley came back to the doorway, he had combed his thick black hair and his shirttail was tucked neatly into his pants.

"Mrs. Mangrum, I didn't know you'd be coming here like this," he said haltingly as he gripped his hands and rubbed the palms together nervously. "If I'd known about it beforehand, I'd had on my good suit and you wouldn't be seeing me look like I am. When I'm not doing my religious work, I'm nothing but an ordinary man."

"Don't you worry about that now, Pastor Purdy," she said as she put her hand on his arm. "You're already beginning to look more like your handsome self again and I feel a lot more sorry for you now than I did before. Now, everything's going to be a lot better for you. I'm going to appreciate you more than ever now in a womanly way and do things for you that a man needs."

"Do you want to come inside and sit down, Mrs. Mangrum, instead of standing out here?"

Glancing behind him at the room, she quickly shook her head. "No, Pastor Purdy. What I came here for was to tell you that I want you to move away from here and come to my house to live. I've got all the spare rooms in the world and I'll fix up a nice one for you."

"But I don't think I could pay—"

"You won't owe me one cent for staying there to sleep, or to eat, either, because it's my own personal way of doing something for you to begin with. When I saw you yesterday, I made up my mind to leave the Methodists and come over to your religion to help you out because I felt sorry for you. Now, you just pack up your belongings and come live with me. The wisdom of fate told me what to do and I'm going to

50

take care of you like one of my own kin and give you all the comforts a fine-looking preacher like you deserves. You won't find a more loving-hearted woman than me all over Augusta when I take a notion to be. I couldn't be more sincere about that. You'll find that out for yourself, Pastor Purdy."

"Are you sure I wouldn't be crowding anybody in your house, Mrs. Mangrum?" he asked. "I don't want the other people in your house to think—"

"It's nobody else's business to think about anything I have a mind to do," she assured him. "It's my house and I run it the way I please and I want a man like you in it. You don't know it, but it's going to be like having my son James come back home to live like I want him to and he won't do."

Smiling gratefully, Raley turned and looked at the bleakness of the room in which he had lived since renting the building for his church three weeks ago. He had collected enough money, going from house to house soliciting contributions, to pay twenty dollars in advance for a month's rent, but after that there was so little money left that he had been living on bread and cheese and, occasionally, a meal of boiled hot dogs.

Since coming to Augusta, he had twice conducted Sunday services, morning and evening each day, but only ten or twelve people had attended the services and the collections had not amounted to enough to be of much help. But even though there had been only five persons present at the previous Wednesday-night prayer meeting, and the collection was only fifty-five cents, he had lost none of his enthusiasm and determination to establish the first church of his Supreme Being Missionary denomination.

While working at a sawmill in East Tennessee, Raley had become inspired with the idea of becoming an evangelist, and since then his ambition had been to create a new religious sect and build chapels and churches all over the South. (*"I'm*

51

going to make everybody take to the new religion and quit the other kind. I want people to listen to me and stop thinking they know better than I do about what's good for them. I've got the true spirit in me now and I've got to tell everybody else how to get it like mine is.") Raley had received his inspiration after listening to a radio broadcast by Billy Graham, who said that he had talked to God and had been told that more evangelists were needed to spread the word that God was not dead and not even sick.

However, Raley realized that it would not be wise to open too many chapels and churches over a large part of the country until the mother church was well-established and self-sustaining. As it was, ever since arriving in Augusta in his ten-year-old automobile, which he had bought in Knoxville for seventy-five dollars, he had constantly hoped and prayed that he would quickly find a wealthy benefactor in the city.

Now that Aimee Mangrum had offered him free room and board, he was quick to grasp her hand, get down on his knees, and kiss the hem of her skirt. While he was on his knees, he closed his eyes and began a long prayer praising Billy Graham for being such a great evangelist and inspiring him over the radio to become an evangelist too. There were tears in Aimee's eyes when he finally finished his prayer and stood up again.

"That affected me just like you'd honestly been proposing marriage to me," she said, wiping the tears from her cheeks. She came closer after that and put her hand on his arm. "Pastor Purdy, it made me flutter all over when you kissed my skirt like that and I can't wait to do something for you. But how come you don't already have a wife to do things for you? A fine-looking manly man like you—"

Embarrassed, his face flushing, he lowered his head and looked down at the floor.

"Well, to tell the truth, I've thought some about getting

married, but I've just never got up enough boldness to make a move like that. A lot of times I get a strong feeling for wanting a woman for what she is, though. Nearly every day lately I've been waking up about five o'clock in the morning with the biggest urge of all about it. It makes me ashamed of myself, but I just can't help myself when it happens."

"You don't have to be ashamed about that, Pastor Purdy," she told him, tenderly patting his arm. "I've been a married woman and I know it can't be helped. It's all right for you to talk to me about it. And when I look at a manly young man like you, I feel so sorry for you that it makes me want to find a way so you can have comfort when you feel the need for it. You just wait, Pastor Purdy. I'm going to keep that in mind for you."

Aimee left him then and started down the steps to the street. Calling to him over her shoulder, she told him to hurry and get ready to move all his belongings to her house.

When she got to the bottom of the steps, she called to him again. "Now, you be sure to get to my house in plenty of time for supper tonight, Pastor Purdy."

Russ had been pacing up and down on the sidewalk while waiting for Aimee, and he got into the car and started the engine before she could open the door on her side and seat herself. They went several blocks out on Sixth Street before either of them spoke.

"Drive to the nearest big supermarket, Russell," she told him then. "I'm going to get a great big load of things to take home to eat. Company's coming to supper tonight and I'm going to have the finest kind of meal for him."

"Who's coming to eat? That preacher you went to see?"

Aimee nodded happily.

"Why do you want to feed him?"

"Because I feel sorry for him."

"I haven't been getting enough to eat myself. All I had this morning was some potatoes and grits and a little dab of greasy sausage. That preacher will hog everything at the table. I know how preachers save up to stuff themselves when they go to somebody else's house. They're all alike. They think the world owes them a living without working for it."

"You won't go hungry anymore from now on, Russell. I'm getting a lot of money and there's going to be plenty to eat for everybody."

She opened her purse and tilted it so he could see the hundred dollars Cato Boykin had given her.

"It's worn-out dirty old money, but I'm going to wash and iron what's left of it after I pay for the groceries."

His face brightened at the first sight of the money in her purse and he slowed down the car in order to look at it more closely a second time.

"Well, Aimee, that makes things a lot different in size and shape," he said. "I've never been bothered how limp and dirty money gets as long as I can buy something with it. Now, I want you to know that I didn't mean to complain about what I said a minute ago. Don't pay any attention to what I said."

Just before reaching the supermarket, Russ leaned close to Aimee and nudged her with a friendly shove of his elbow.

"Aimee, I'm thinking that you'd like to know that I need a set of new tires for my car. I've been wanting to tell you, but I hated to bother you about it before. It's real dangerous driving on these worn-out old tires. Real dangerous. They're so bald-headed they're liable to blow out any minute and somebody could get hurt real bad. It's exactly what I saw happen last night when I was on my way to bowling. A nice lady about your own age got killed right in the middle of the expressway and it was a terrible thing to see happen because of worn-out old tires on her car."

"You wait here in front of the store till I pick out all the groceries I want and bring them to the car," she told him when he stopped at the supermarket. "Then you drive this car slow and careful like you ought to all the way home and nobody'll get hurt."

After spending nearly an hour in the supermarket, Aimee had bought enough food to fill three grocery carts. When everything had been put into the car, they drove slowly home while Russ whistled to himself in good spirits all the way.

In the late afternoon, after having spent a long time preparing one of the vacant rooms for Raley Purdy, Aimee was too excited to sleep when she lay down for her usual afternoon nap. She got up after a restless half-hour on her bed and went down to the veranda to wait for Raley to get there.

Before going down, Aimee had taken off the green dress she had worn since early morning and had put on her favorite pink cotton dress, which had a lower neckline than any of the others she had made. She had also fluffed her graying hair more carefully than she did ordinarily and put more coloring on her cheeks than she had done in several years.

Aimee had seated herself in one of the large veranda chairs and tried to remain calm by forcing herself to keep from looking up the road every few minutes to see if Raley was coming.

The monotonous grinding hum of the huge yellow bull-dozer scraping and terracing the earth on the other side of Mangrum Road was annoying, but she tried to ignore the sound so she could remain unruffled and be in a pleasant mood when Raley arrived. A breeze was blowing the fumes from the diesel engine directly to the veranda and she waved the irritating odor away by fanning her face with her hand.

After sitting calmly and patiently on the veranda for nearly an hour, hoping every minute to see Raley drive up to the house in his car, Aimee finally got up from her chair and tried to see as far as she could up Mangrum Road in the direction of the expressway.

However, there was no automobile within sight, and she began to worry about the possibility that Raley had forgotten how to get to her house and was helplessly lost somewhere between Reynolds Street and Mangrum Road. It was nearly five o'clock by then and she thought of giving Graham some money to buy gasoline and sending him to look for Raley.

While she stood there trying to decide what she should do, she saw an automobile coming down the road from the expressway at an unusually fast speed. A few moments later, the car suddenly slowed down, and then it turned into the driveway and stopped in front of the house. Aimee could see a taxi sign on the roof of the brightly painted blue-and-white car and she wondered why Raley had not come in his own car and saved the cost of the taxi fare.

While she waited at the veranda railing to see Raley get out of the taxi, she saw a young woman step to the ground instead. After handing some money to the driver, the young woman leaned through the window and said something to him. Both of them were laughing as she picked up her suitcase and started up the walkway.

Aimee did not recognize the younger of her two daughters until she saw Connie's bright blonde hair and long slender legs. Connie had been away for nearly two years and Aimee had had no idea where she was during all that time.

Just before Connie got to the veranda steps, the taxi driver blew the horn three short beeps, and she turned around and waved friendlily as he drove away. Connie was dressed just as Aimee would have expected her to be. She had always been particular about her clothes and long before she left home to find a job somewhere, had constantly studied fashion magazines and compared patterns. And now, after having been away all that time, she was even more striking in appearance as she came up the steps with her same expressive smile. Connie's expensive dress, jewelry, and handbag looked as if they had just been bought at a fashionable style showing.

"Connie—my little baby girl!" Aimee exclaimed.

"Hello, Mamma," Connie said, putting down her suitcase when she reached the veranda. "Did I surprise you? It's so good to see you again, Mamma."

"Where have you been all this time, honey?"

"I've been in Savannah."

"But that's so close—you could've come home a lot sooner. I thought you'd gone to the other side of the world."

Aimee gripped her shoulders with both hands and held her at arms' length.

"I can't believe it, honey!" Aimee said with tears coming to her eyes. The next moment she had put her arms around Connie and began sobbing. "You're here now! My own little baby girl! I felt so sorry for you being off all alone by yourself all this time! I thought I'd never live to see you again! I could feel myself getting old and sick and never knowing what minute I'd die! I'm so glad you're here right now and have come back to stay!"

"I'm glad to be here, too, Mamma," Connie told her. "But I'll be here for only just a little while."

"Don't say that, honey!"

With a gasp, Aimee held her breath as long as she could. Then she began weeping again.

"Don't break my heart! I can't stand hearing you say that, honey! I won't live much longer at my age! Don't go away when I'm going to die! Please don't ever leave home again!"

"You mustn't be like this now, Mamma," Connie said soothingly. "We can talk about it later. Now, tell me all about you. And how is everybody else? Are Velma and Woody still living here? And Uncle Russ? What about Graham?"

Aimee wiped the tears from her cheeks.

"Honey, everything's just like it's always been. We're still your loving homefolks. And we've missed you every minute of the time for almost two years now. It's been awful not having you at home. Please say you won't never go away again and leave me. You're the only baby girl I'll ever have and I'll be too lonesome from now on without you in the house."

"What about Jim?" Connie asked quickly. "Has he been here to see you lately?"

"He has not! No more than he's ever done since he left home and went away the first time. I don't like to say it about my own son, but James is too peculiar to be a real Mangrum like the rest of us. He's more like an outsider than a Mangrum. He even acts like he's ashamed to be one of us. He still won't come to visit more than once or twice a year. And then when he does come, he gets real provoked at me when I won't listen to him and sell our homeplace and move away to live in a city apartment like he wants me to.

"And another thing. James still won't even spend the night in our own house. When I beg him to, he says he left home for good and is never going to sleep here again even one night. I'm proud of James being a doctor in a big city like Atlanta, if I have to admit it—and sometimes I do like to boast about it—but I'll never forgive him for being peculiar and not a home-loving Mangrum like the rest of us. What ruined James was going away to college ten years ago and getting his peculiar notions. Cato Boykin won't admit it, but I'm suspicious that he loaned James money to go off to college and medical school. And Dr. Price may have had something to do with it, too. That makes me suspicious of both of them. Anyway, James won't come back home to live with me. He's the only Mangrum I've ever had to criticize for that."

Having heard the blowing of the taxi horn and then Aimee's excited voice as she greeted Connie, Russ and Katie had already got to the veranda and Velma and Woody were coming through the doorway. Graham was the last to get there.

While all of them were crowding around Connie and trying to talk at the same time, there was a startling, noisy rattle of metal as Raley Purdy's car crashed head-on into one of the big oak trees while he was trying to steer the car around the unfamiliar circular driveway. An instant later there was a loud hissing of steam and a deafening backfire from the exhaust pipe.

After the crash, Raley tried to start the engine of his mud-splashed car in order to back away from the tree, but all it did was sputter weakly several times and then quit completely. He got out of the car and came toward the house, carrying a large cardboard box piled high with his belongings.

"It's Pastor Purdy at last!" Aimee exclaimed happily. She left Connie and went to the top of the steps to greet him. "I was worrying myself sick about Pastor Purdy just a little while ago. I was so afraid he'd got lost somewhere looking for me and never would find his way here."

"What's he coming here for with that box he's carrying?" Woody asked Russ.

"He's moving in," Russ told him.

"The hell you say! Another eater?"

"Sure. He prayed for free room and board and Aimee provided. And she did it a lot quicker than God could do it."

"If he eats here just once, he'll start praying to God for Miss Mamma Aimee to provide more lean meat in the sausage when the lard starts running out his ears."

Aimee was waiting for Raley when he came up the steps to the veranda. She welcomed him by immediately grasping his arm before he could put down the heavy box and then led him toward the doorway while motioning for the others to stand aside and let them pass.

"There's no time to stop now and talk," she said, pausing at the door and smiling happily. "There'll be plenty of time later on for everybody to get personally acquainted. I'm going to take Pastor Purdy straight up to his room right away and help him get settled and made comfortable. I want him to feel right at home at the start and not like a total stranger. He's been living a pitiful life on Reynolds Street for the past three weeks with nobody to take good care of him."

Still grasping Raley's arm, Aimee beckoned urgingly to Connie with a fluttering of her other hand.

"Come on upstairs with us, honey. It just had to be the wisdom of fate that told me to do it, because I fixed up the bedroom for Pastor Purdy that's side-by-side with your own girlhood room. You and him will be right there where you can get personally acquainted a lot better than some other places in the house where you wouldn't have the same privacy. I couldn't have arranged it better even if I'd known beforehand that you'd be coming home like this at the very same time that Pastor Purdy was moving in. No matter what happens, it proves that the wisdom of fate always knows best."

After the three of them had gone into the house, Woody Woodruff got his guitar and began fingering the strings and carefully tuning it to his satisfaction. When he finished, he straddled the veranda railing and sat there, looking across the yard at the paint-faded, fender-dented, four old automobiles in the driveway.

Velma, who had been sitting on the settee, got up and came to the railing.

"What's the matter, Woody?" she asked. "You look worried. What is it?"

He put his arm around her neck and hugged her.

"I'm stuck, baby," he said. "I'm absolutely stuck-stuck. I can't picture what to do. I keep on hearing two songs."

"Tell me what you hear, Woody."

Lowering his head over the guitar, he listened closely to the sound of his musical notes. When he straightened up, he pointed toward the driveway.

"One of them is about being lucky to have a home in Miss

Mamma Aimee's old rusty used-car lot and the other one is about a downtown gal getting set for a big rumble with a long-legged Tennessee preacher."

"Do both of them, Woody," Velma begged, snuggling against him. "I want to hear them. They'll both be wonderful the way you make up songs."

Chapter 7

It was long after dark by the time supper was over and everybody had left the dining room. When Martha came from the kitchen, before stacking the dirty plates and dishes she slapped the table with her damp towel several times, as if she hoped some of them would get broken so they could be thrown away and not have to be washed.

Earlier, when Aimee had come to the kitchen to urge her to hurry supper, Martha had tried to complain about having to cook for two more people in the house, but Aimee, refusing to listen, had walked away holding her hands against her ears.

Velma and Woody, having hurried through supper, had already left for the Midnight Go-Go Club on Fort Gordon

Highway, where Woody and the other two musicians of the combo had a job for the weekend and were to be paid fifty dollars each for the three-night engagement. Katie and Russ went upstairs to their room to watch a favorite television program and all the others were in the parlor, where the windows had been closed to keep out the sickening odor of the miasma that was rising from the swampy lowland around the pond.

Connie, her bright blonde hair sparkling in the parlor lights, had changed her clothes before supper and she was wearing a thin black dress that was too short to cover her knees and designed so that it only partly covered her prominent breasts. She was sitting in a comfortable chair in front of her mother and Raley Purdy and listening occasionally to what her mother was saying.

Each time Raley looked at Connie, she regarded him with an encouraging smile until he became embarrassed by her boldness and looked away from her. He had already tried several times to ease his discomfort by thrusting his hands between his legs and pressing his knees tightly together. Connie had a way of looking directly at him and raising her eyebrows slightly each time that happened.

On the far side of the parlor near the door, Graham was slumped deeply in his chair. With a glowering scowl, he frequently stared across the room at Raley sitting close to his mother. Graham had been sullen and morose ever since his mother had seated Raley beside her at the dining-room table. What he also resented was that his mother had served Raley first with generous helpings from the serving dishes. Then by the time the dishes were passed to him at the other end of the table there was not enough food left for him to have his usual large portions.

"I've always wanted to have true happiness in life," Aimee

said after a deep sigh, "and I never had anything like it in all my life till you brought it to me, Pastor Purdy."

Although Raley appeared to be trying to pay attention to what Aimee was saying, he became distracted when he turned his head and looked at Connie's long slender legs below her short skirt and then saw the startling bareness of her breasts above the top of the thin black dress. After that, when he was not thrusting his hands into his lap, he would be restlessly crossing and recrossing his long lean legs. Whenever he glanced at Connie to see if she had noticed what he was doing, she would look at him with a favoring smile.

"I couldn't be more sincere about my happiness now, Pastor Purdy," Aimee continued. "I had a sort of old makeshift kind of happiness with the Methodists, but it was a poor substitute for the true kind. The preacher at the Methodist church is an ordinary-looking old somebody and he has a spiteful little old dried-up wife who acts like she's getting ready to spit in my face every time I try to get him aside and talk to him privately about my religion. You know how spiteful a preacher's wife can be, don't you, Pastor Purdy?"

"Yes, yes!" he said quickly, startled by the sound of his own name. "That's very true, Mrs. Mangrum."

"But when you came along, Pastor Purdy, I said to myself, uh-huh, it's the wisdom of fate bringing me true happiness at last. That was right out there at the front door the first time I laid eyes on you. I was so inspired by the manly way you looked that I felt sorry for you right away and tingled all over with happiness like I've never done around that ordinary-looking Methodist preacher and his spiteful wife.

"You maybe didn't know about it at the time, Pastor Purdy, but when I saw you first of all I wanted to reach out and touch you and do something for you right away. Like I said, that was the first time I saw you and I was too flustered then to speak up and ask you what you wanted me to do for you beside giving you the little money I had in my purse. But if you'd said you wanted me to lift up my skirt for you, I'd gone right ahead and done it."

"Mamma!" Connie spoke to her sharply.

Aimee hastily covered her mouth with both hands.

"I got carried away," she said after a moment. "But it shows how earnest I am and I don't mind being known for that."

Raley looked down at the floor and restlessly crossed his legs again.

"Anyhow," Aimee continued after that, clasping her hands on her lap and smiling at Raley, "anyhow, I've felt that way ever since and I wouldn't be sincere if I didn't say so and tried to hide my true feelings. A lot of women try to hide their true feelings about a man they're sorry for and they'll pretend something else entirely different instead of going ahead and doing something for him. But not me. You can count on that. I'm a sincere woman about my personal feelings. I come right out in the open and say it in plain words so you'll know how anxious I am to do something for you, Pastor Purdy. I might not look it now, but I know all about the kind of personal attention a man needs. I haven't lived my life without finding that out."

"Mamma, why don't you let him say something? You're doing all the talking."

"It's all right with me for her to keep on," Raley was quick to say. "I don't have nothing to say, anyhow."

"Then to get back to what I was talking about a while ago," Aimee went on. "I'll always remember the time I first laid eyes on you, Pastor Purdy. I couldn't've been more thrilled if I'd been an innocent young girl all alone somewhere in the dark with a man for the first time and wanting to find out what he was going to do next. And now that I feel so much happiness with you coming to live right here in the same house with me, I'm going to make a special effort to do everything for you, Pastor Purdy. I'm going to look after you day and night and you won't never have to worry about not getting the kind of attention you want."

Aimee reached for Raley's arm and pulled him closer.

"It makes me excited just to talk about it. Don't you feel good about it already, Pastor Purdy? And wasn't it the wisdom of fate for my little baby girl to come home at the same time you moved in to live? I couldn't think of a better romantic thing to happen. What I want to see now is you and her have the nicest kind of time getting personally acquainted."

Graham, looking sullen and resentful, got up and left the room. He could be heard stomping heavily through the hall and then banging the screen door when he went out to the veranda.

With her round pink face glowing, Aimee gently began to pat Raley's arm. By that time, Raley was unable to keep from staring longingly at Connie. Suddenly he sat up erectly in his chair as if he could not control himself any longer and had to leave the house and go to the front yard to take a walk in the night. Before he could leave, though, Aimee tightened her grip on his arm and began talking again.

"Maybe you don't know it, honey," she said to Connie, leaning closer and lowering her voice intimately, "but Pastor Purdy has been so busy getting his new church started that he's never had time to get to know somebody like you in a personal way. That's a dreadful shame. When he told me he's never been married, I said to myself, uh-huh, because I felt so sorry for him that all I could think about was wanting to do something for him to hurry up and make up for it. That's when I decided not to let him keep on being miserable any longer than I could help it. And now that you're here—"

"Mamma," Connie interrupted with a lifting of her voice, "you don't have to keep on talking like that. It's not necessary. He's a man. He can take care of himself if he wants to."

66

Raley tried again to get up and leave, but Aimee kept a tight grip on his arm.

"Well, honey, then all I ask is that you make it easy for him. I know you can be real nice to him and let him find from you what it's like to get the attention he's missed so far. He's a deserving man and that's why I've felt sorry for him from the start. It's a rare thing to come across a deserving man like him who's saved up all this time for a woman's attention. You've been living down in Savannah for nearly two years and you're bound to be acquainted with some of the men down there. But Pastor Purdy's not ordinary like other men. That's why I want you to make it easy for him at the start. You can get the feeling of how different he is just by being around him like right now. So just remember that you're not married yet, either, and might want to start thinking about it for the near future. It wouldn't be like a Mangrum to stay single all your life."

"What about Graham? He's not married."

"Graham's different that way. He's not suited to leave home and go off in the world by himself. He needs to stay here and have my protection. It'd break my heart if Graham went off and lived with some woman who wouldn't go to the trouble to take care of him like I do. And besides, I need one member of the family to be sure to stay here with me. I couldn't bear to be left all alone in the world."

Unable to sit still any longer, Raley got up and pulled his arm from Aimee's grasp. Then, walking stiff-legged in long strides, he went through the hall and down the veranda steps to the front yard. Graham shouted something to him from the veranda, but nothing was heard from Raley.

"We'll excuse Pastor Purdy for getting up and leaving us like that to go think," Aimee told Connie. "I could tell by the way he acted that he couldn't wait another minute to go outside and walk around by himself to do some thinking. He's a real thinking man and that's another thing I admire so much about him. Now, honey, I want to hear all about what you've been doing down in Savannah for nearly two years, but it's getting real late for me to be up and that'll have to wait till tomorrow. I know you've got a lot to tell me."

"There's not much to tell you, Mamma. I've been working recently in a private club. It's closed down now for two weeks and then it'll reopen in a new place. That's why I could come home for a vacation."

Aimee's face brightened with curiosity.

"What kind of a private club, honey? Is it like the Elks and the Moose?"

"Not exactly, but it is a club for men only."

"If it's a place for men only, what in the world would you be doing there?"

"What I mean is that no outside women or wives are admitted."

"Then what do you do in a place like that?"

"I'm a hostess. Three of us work there like that."

Aimee, frowning, thought with a shaking of her head.

"I hope you won't say you're nothing but a common waitress, honey. The Mangrums have never been anybody's servants. We have too much family pride for that. We've always hired ordinary colored people to do servant work for us. That's what they are for."

"Being a hostess is different."

"How is it different?"

"We serve drinks from the bar and dance with the members and talk to them and just be sociable in general."

"And you said their wives don't go there for that."

"Only the hostesses are there."

"Then how sociable do you get where there's men only like that?" Aimee asked pointedly.

Connie smiled. "It all depends."

Aimee nodded briefly.

"Is that dress you've got on now the kind you wear being a hostess?"

"No. This is one I wear when I go somewhere else on a date. We wear very informal little costumes at the club."

"I've seen pictures of what you might be talking about and some of them are next-to-nothing. Some of them show off a woman just like she was standing there natural. But everybody knows that's what men go around looking for."

Aimee looked closely at Connie for several moments before speaking again.

"Do you go to bed with men, honey?" she asked with an intimate lowering of her voice. "Tell me the truth about it. I'm your mother. You can confide in me. Tell me all about it. It'll do both of us a lot of good for you to tell me. I never had a chance to talk to you about it before and now is a good time to do it. Now, honey, do you do that?"

"It all depends."

Aimee leaned back in her chair with a satisfied sigh, nodding to herself as though she had been told exactly what she had expected to hear.

Before anything else was said, they heard Graham shouting in a loud voice on the veranda. If Raley himself said anything, he was too far away to be heard in the parlor.

"I'm so glad we can have mother-daughter talk in a personal way like this," Aimee said presently. "Talking in confidence about sleeping with men can do a lot of good. I always thought it was no harm for some unmarried girls to do that for special occasions, because men expect it and they've got to be pleased in their own natural way. If a girl won't listen to a man with that on his mind, he's liable to walk off and you'll never see him again. That's why a girl has to learn early in life what to do about what men want or she'll run the risk of being passed by and never get a man to marry her. Of course, men don't always want to get married and they'd rather give

69

presents instead. Is that how you got all your fine clothes, honey?"

"I earn a good salary, Mamma."

Aimee bit her lip thoughtfully for a moment. "I suppose it's only natural for a girl to take presents when you're around men who admire you—no matter how much money you earn working. And being a Mangrum and as pretty as you are—"

"Some men say they like me better than the other two girls at the club because I am a Mangrum."

"I'm glad to hear that and I'm not a bit surprised. Any worthwhile man ought to appreciate a girl who has the Mangrum family name. I'd scorn any man who didn't appreciate you and wouldn't do more for you because of who you are. If he didn't, he wouldn't be worth wiping your feet on."

"Well, nearly everybody at the club seems to know about the family."

"Everybody should know about us. And if somebody says he don't, then he won't deserve to. The Mangrums have always been prominent people, I'm proud to say. You ask anybody in Augusta and Richmond County about us. They'll tell you what a prominent family we are. It proved what people think of us when they named a fine big new schoolhouse for your grandfather Alexander Mangrum, and then there's Mangrum Road and Mangrum Creek named for us, too. Not to mention that big statue near the courthouse with your great-grandfather Maury Mangrum sitting on a prancing horse like the war hero he was.

"I just can't stop talking about the Mangrums when I get started like this—we've always owned a lot of property, and we're educated people, too. There's not many women in Augusta who can boast about graduating from Miss Sutton's School up there on The Hill like I did. Then you and Velma came along and went all the way through high school—not to mention James going to the university and getting to be a

70

well-known doctor in Atlanta. Of course, Graham couldn't get a full education, because he could stay in grammar school only a few years, but that's because he's different.

"I could go on talking about the Mangrums all night, honey, because there's so much to say about us. We've been prominent people ever since the first Mangrum got here from Europe and bought up thousands and thousands of acres of plantation land and started our family. I can say that with pride because I was a Mangrum myself even before I married your father. That makes me a double-Mangrum and all the better for it. Some people will say first cousins shouldn't marry and have children for some silly reason or other, like me and your father did, but it was better to do that than marry somebody outside the Mangrum family who had only common ordinary ancestry like most people do. That's why we have more family pride than anybody else. And I don't never want to hear of some man looking at you and not appreciating you like he ought to, neither."

Aimee had been talking so excitedly that she was out of breath and she had to wait several moments before she could say anything more.

"When I get started talking about the pride I have in the Mangrums, it's such a pleasant feeling that it's hard for me to quit," she said, her eyes misty and blinking. Then leaning closer to Connie, Aimee patted her knee. "But there's something else important I want to tell you, honey. Don't you dare say a word to Pastor Purdy about what we talked about confidentially a while ago. We'll keep all that to ourselves. That kind of woman-talk ought to be kept a secret from men, because they're liable to get upset if they know about some of the things women talk about naturally when we're by ourselves. That's why I don't want Pastor Purdy to know about it. There's some things men don't understand about women and he'd be too upset to come anywhere near you and look you straight in the face if he found out about you down in Savannah. I don't want that to happen for his sake. It'd spoil everything I'm planning for him. It'd be just too much for him to think about and worry over."

"What are you planning for him, Mamma?" Connie asked.

"Well, that's not something to talk about right now, because I'm still working it out in my mind."

"Are you thinking about marrying him?"

"Me?" She pressed her hands against her round pink face. "What makes you think that? Don't you think he'd rather have a young girl your age?"

Aimee had been so absorbed in talking about the Mangrums and so concerned about what could be done for Raley Purdy that she had not asked any more questions about the place in Savannah where Connie was a hostess. What Connie had not told her mother about the Select Club was that it had several gambling tables and an after-hours bar and couch rooms on the second floor.

The Select Club had been raided by the police following a complaint made by the wife of one of the customers and all the furnishings had either been confiscated or destroyed. However, no arrests resulted from the raid and an agreement had been made that the club would not reopen anywhere in the city if the charges against it for permitting gambling and prostitution were dropped and not brought to court. As it was, an arrangement had been made to reopen the club at a new location in the county which was just a few blocks beyond the city limits. The club manager had told Connie and the other two hosesses, Jean and Elaine, to leave town to avoid the newspaper reporters, who were still trying to find out more about the operation of the club, and to stay away until it was ready to reopen in the county location. Jean and Elaine had gone to Jacksonville, where they had worked before coming to Savannah.

Aimee, getting up from her chair with laborious effort, took a few steps toward the door and then stopped and carefully smoothed the creases that had wrinkled her dress. It was already after midnight by then and she sleepily rubbed her face with both hands.

"It's getting so real late and past my bedtime and I've talked myself hoarse. I'll bet I sound like an old bullfrog who's been croaking all night out there at the pond. I had so much of importance to say, though, I just couldn't quit talking on and on. It's been so long since I've seen you, honey, that I had a thousand things to say. I don't know when I've had such a good time talking with somebody to listen to me. Velma stays around Woody Woodruff all the time and hardly comes near me to listen to what I want to talk about and I wouldn't open my mouth to Katie and say one word I don't have to. Talking to you tonight, honey, has done me more good than a whole dose of Dr. Price's medicine."

She rubbed her face again and went as far as the door.

"I'm going to bed now, honey. You just stay right here till Pastor Purdy comes back and then you and him can be all alone by yourselves. Young people like you and him have all the time in the world to stay up late and get personally acquainted. Now, you be real nice to him like a girl can when she tries. He deserves all the attention you can give a man and I want you to do that for him for my sake. When you get to know him, you'll feel sorry for him just like I do and want to do something for him."

"I'm going upstairs, too," Connie said. "He'll know where to find me if he wants to."

"Well, it'll make it a lot easier for him if you'll leave your door open just a little bit and the light turned on. I don't know about the kind of men you're accustomed to in Savannah, but he's awfully shy and timid. He's the kind who needs to be coaxed some and helped along at the start and then

73

there's no holding back that kind from then on. I can still size up a man at my age and I could tell that about Pastor Purdy the first time I saw him. If you haven't found that out already about some men, you'll be learning it from him."

Turning off the parlor lights, Aimee and Connie went upstairs together. Nothing more was said until they were at the door of Connie's room.

"What should I call him, Mamma?" she asked as Aimee went toward her room. "I'd feel silly calling him Pastor Purdy like you do. I'd never get used to it."

"Call him Raley, of course. That's the suitable thing under the circumstances. It wouldn't sound dignified if I do it, but you can. You and him are at the right age to call each other by first names for quick acquaintance and save a lot of time."

Chapter 8

Connie went into her room, leaving the door partly open, and turned on the lights and began taking off her clothes. When she had finished undressing, she went to the window. The late-night breeze was blowing the miasma away from the house and the croaker frogs at the pond had quieted down in the cooler air. It was the time of year when the humid heat of summer was still a month away and the evenings were comfortable between midnight and dawn.

As she stood at the window looking into the darkness, she remembered the nights in spring and summer while she was still in high school when she had often slept on a settee on the veranda with only a light blanket for covering. (*The thing about Connie Mangrum is that she should've left home long before she did and that could've kept her out of the trouble she got into in Augusta. Her mother still doesn't know about it, but the police haven't forgotten, and a lot of other people remember, too. Aimee Mangrum wouldn't let her go away to college when she graduated from high school. In no time at all she was a pick-up around town and that could've been her way of getting even with her mother. The police were good to her for a while, because she was a Mangrum, but finally they had to tell her to leave Augusta or they'd have to arrest her the next time. Of course, if she'd started out being a careful call-girl, it might've been different. But that wasn't what she wanted. What she must have had in mind was to get even with her mother for not letting her go away to college by being a common pick-up hanging around the corner of Eighth and Ellis. However, the way it was, Aimee Mangrum never knew about it, but nearly everybody else did.)* While Connie was thinking about taking a blanket down to the veranda this time, she remembered that Graham was still there and she decided to wait in her room.

As she waited at the window, she wondered if Raley would be in the yard where he could see her. She knew then that she was going to be disappointed if he did not come to her room and went to his own room instead and locked the door. For a while, she wondered if she should go to his room and let him find her in his bed. However, she decided that she would rather stay where she was and have him come to her.

After listening to her mother talk about Raley and remembering the eager way he had looked at her in the parlor, she was more curious than ever to find out what kind of man he would be with her when they were alone. The men she had known in Savannah were married and impassive and it had been a long time since she had been with a man who was wildly enthusiastic and exciting.

As if he had been waiting in the yard for Connie to go to

76

her room and turn on the light, Raley came back into the house. Graham shouted something to him when he crossed the veranda and went into the hall, but Raley went straight to the stairway without speaking and climbed the steps two at a time.

Connie had left the window when she heard Raley come into the house and she was standing at the foot of her bed when he passed the partly opened door on the way to his room. She knew he had seen her, because he had paused momentarily to stare at her before disappearing from sight. Connie waited, listening for the sound of the opening and closing of his door, but instead there was silence in the house.

Going to her door then, she waited behind it, out of sight from the hall. Presently, tiptoeing cautiously, Raley came back to the door and slowly craned his neck until he could see into the room again. When he did not see Connie at the foot of the bed, he stepped all the way into the room. He still had not seen Connie when she quickly closed the door behind him and locked it.

Startled by what had happened, he turned around with a nervous twisting of his body. When he saw that she was naked, he tried to reach for the doorknob. Connie moved in front of him and he quickly jerked his hand away to keep from touching her.

"Look here!" he said in a hoarse whisper. "You don't have your clothes on! You're naked all over!"

She reached up and stroked her bright blonde hair away from her face.

"Do you like me the way I am?"

"But you're naked—naked all over!"

"I thought you wanted to see me like this."

"But it's different—I didn't know you'd be so naked—"

"But the way you were looking at me in the parlor to-night—wasn't that what you were thinking about?"

77

"I don't know—now."

He moved backward several steps.

"Raley, wouldn't you like to put your arms around me and hold me tight?"

She saw him looking at her breasts and she moved closer to him.

"Wouldn't you? It's what I want you to do."

"But it's not right," he protested with nervous motions of his head while running his fingers through his hair. "I can't do that—it wouldn't be right."

"Why not?" she said, moving another step closer.

"I don't know—but I shouldn't—"

"But you want to, don't you, Raley?"

"Yes—but it still wouldn't be right."

"Not even if I say it's all right?"

He wet his dry lips with his tongue.

"A good girl—she wouldn't—"

"Wouldn't what?"

"Well, with the lights turned on—"

"But you wouldn't see me in the dark. And I couldn't see you, either."

"Me? See me? But I've got my clothes on!"

"Raley, tell me the truth," Connie said, turning her body first to one side and then to the other. "Don't you like to look at me the way I am now? Wasn't that what you were thinking about when you were looking at me in the parlor?"

Appearing to be trying to think what to say, he again nervously wet his dry lips. Connie looked at his long legs and lean hips and then at his flushed face. Seeing that he was boldly looking at her breasts at last, she pushed them upward as she went closer to him so he would let himself touch her. Raley stepped backward, though still entranced by the sight of her breasts, until he was at the foot of the bed.

"There's nothing to worry about any longer, Raley," she

said helpfully as she went to him and began unbuttoning his shirt. At first he tried to stop her by holding his arms over his chest, but soon his trembling hands fell weakly at his sides. "Don't be afraid, Raley. It's all right. I know what to do. And I wouldn't be here doing this if I didn't want to. Can't you tell? You don't have to be afraid any longer."

"What are you doing to me?" he said in a hoarse whisper as Connie put her hand under his shirt and began stroking his chest with the tips of her fingers. "It feels like—like—I don't know!"

When Connie did not say anything, he suddenly drew in his breath and held it as long as he could.

"Somebody might find out about me," he said fearfully as soon as he began breathing again. "That's what I'm scared about. If somebody found out that I was here like this—if somebody saw me now—saw what you're doing—if Billy Graham saw me now—Billy Graham would—"

"Billy Graham?" Connie said, tossing her bright blonde hair away from her face. "Who's Billy Graham? And what's he got to do with it?"

"Everybody knows Billy Graham—Billy Graham has his radio program on every Sunday that everybody listens to."

"I've listened to a lot of disc jockeys but I don't remember anybody with that name. His name sounds all right, though. What's his specialty? Is he rock-and-roll, country, or pop? What's his radio station?"

"Billy Graham's everywhere on radio stations all over the country. He's everywhere like God is. If you'll put your clothes on, I'll tell you what a great evangelist Billy Graham is. I can't talk about Billy Graham when you're naked—he wouldn't want me to."

"Is that so?" Connie said with a puzzled look. "I don't know what it's all about. What are you trying to tell me, anyway?

Billy Graham—Billy Graham! Are you trying to tell me you've never had a girl down the middle before? Is that it?"

"We're not married—and you're naked—that's why—and Billy Graham said he didn't even kiss his wife until after they got engaged. Billy Graham wouldn't—"

"Wait a minute, Raley," she said, smiling about his wanting her to put on her dress. "That sounds like homo talk. You can get engaged and marry somebody some other time. You don't have to be married now."

Connie finished unbuttoning his shirt and threw it aside with the top of his underwear. Standing there as if he had been stunned by a blow on the head while he felt the caressing touch of her hands and lips on his chest, he made no effort after that to stop her when she unbuckled his belt and pushed his pants and the rest of his underwear down to his ankles. Looking at him at last in all his nakedness as she wanted to see him, Connie got down on her knees and put her hands around the long throbbing prong of his body and kissed him with the fullness of her mouth. Hobbled by the clothing around his ankles, the only movement he could make was to sit down on the bed. It was then that she pulled the rest of his clothes from his legs and he reached for her body and put his hands on her for the first time.

She leaned over him then, pushing him downward, and rubbed the softness of her flesh on the hardness of his body while he squirmed with the pain of her fingernails digging into him.

"Let me up!" he said, loud and hoarse, as he tried to push her away. "I've got to get up!"

"Get up for what?"

"I want to pray—I can't pray like this!"

She hit his face with a stinging slap.

"You bastard! Let Billy Graham pray for you!"

His whole body began trembling and she felt the frantic

80

clutching of his hands on her breasts and buttocks. She waited until he kissed her, and then she wrapped the warmth of her body around him to get the ecstacy she wanted.

Suddenly there was a pounding on the door and they heard Graham, his angry voice loud and demanding, calling to Connie to unlock the door and let him into the room.

"That preacher's in there!" Graham shouted. "He's nowhere else in the house and I saw him come inside! I know what he's doing! I don't want him to! Make him stop and let me in! You hear me, Connie?"

"Go away, Graham!" she called to him.

"You can't make me! I want in there!"

Connie lay still, hoping her brother would leave any moment, but after a short interval of silence he began kicking the door.

Flushed and angry then, Connie sat on the side of the bed and with both hands tried to brush her tousled blonde hair into place. Listening to the kicking on the door and fearful that Graham would knock it down and come into the room at any moment, Raley grasped his still erect prong protectingly as he crouched on the bed.

"They found out," Raley said in a whisper quavering with anxiety. "They've got the same name—Graham—Graham—and if Billy Graham saw me like this now—I can't hide it—"

"If you don't hurry up and unlock the door, I'll break it down," Graham warned her. "I know what he's in there for. You'd better make him stop and open the door."

Raley got up from the bed and looked wildly around the room for some way to hide or escape.

"Stop that and go away and leave me alone, Graham," Connie told her brother. "You've got no right to come in here. Now go away like I told you."

Raley, crouching to protect himself, went from one side of the room to the other.

"You can't make me go away. And if you don't let me in, I'll break down the door. I know what that preacher's in there for."

Graham began kicking the door harder than ever.

Connie knew that Graham would find Raley if he tried to hide under the bed or in the closet and she picked up his clothing and shoved it at him. Moving in haste, Raley climbed through the window and stepped out of sight to the porch roof below. She stood at the window while he crawled to the edge of the roof and then waited until she heard him drop to the ground.

"You'd better let me in," Graham warned her.

"All right," Connie said calmly. "I'll unlock it, Graham. Wait just a minute now."

She quickly put on the first dress she could find and then unlocked the door.

When the door was unlocked, Graham ran past her into the room. He looked first at the rumpled sheets and then got down on his knees and looked under the bed. After opening the closet door and looking inside, he slammed it shut and went to the window.

"You let him get away, didn't you?"

Connie said nothing.

Graham was still leaning through the window and looking for Raley in the darkness when Aimee, tottering sleepily and with her faded green bathrobe wrapped loosely around her, came into the room with her eyes blinking in the bright light. A moment later, Katie and Russ, clutching their night clothes around them, got to the door.

"What in the world is going on here?" Aimee said. "I never heard so much shouting and banging going on at this time of night. It's after two o'clock in the morning."

"Look there, Mamma," Graham said, leaving the window and pointing at the rumpled sheets on the bed. "See that?

That preacher was in here and he was on the bed with her. I knew he was in here, but Connie wouldn't unlock the door in time and he got out through the window before I could catch him. I'd cut his balls off if I'd caught him. But I'll get even with him yet."

"Now, Graham," Aimee said soothingly as she patted his arm. "Don't get upset and say things like that. It's nothing to carry on that way about at this time of night. Just calm down now. Pastor Purdy is a fine man and I don't want him harmed."

"But she had him in here and he was on the bed with her, Mamma. Look at the bed—you can tell. If she told the truth, she'd have to say she was letting him do it."

"You mustn't talk that way about your sister, Graham. It's not a nice way to behave."

"You're taking up for her," he said accusingly. "You're just like she is. You let him do anything he wants—you gave him big helpings at the table—you let him sit right next to you in the dining room—"

"Graham," she spoke to him patiently, "I won't like you if you keep on talking that way. You want me to like you, don't you? Now, if you didn't see Pastor Purdy in here, then there's nothing to be upset about."

"Then why ain't he in his own room right now like he ought to be? I saw him come in the house. And before that I saw how he was looking at her down in the parlor. He was just waiting for a chance to come in here and get on the bed with her."

"I don't like to hear Pastor Purdy criticized like that, Graham. He's the kind of man who likes to do a lot of thinking and I expect he went back outside again to do just that. Maybe you didn't see him leave because he could've gone out again through the kitchen door instead of the front. It's just like him to be walking around right now somewhere outside in the night thinking. He's the kind of man who spends a lot of his time thinking about things. Now, Graham, you go on to your room and get a good night's sleep. I don't want you to stay here and upset your sister and spoil her homecoming by talking like you've been doing. You do like I say so I'll like you. Everything'll be all right in the morning."

"How do I know he won't come back in here again?"

"He went outside to think and I expect he'll be busy thinking the rest of the night."

Velma and Woody, getting back from the nightclub, came down the lighted hall to where Katie and Russ were standing outside Connie's room. Before anything was said, Graham came stomping through the doorway and shoved Woody aside with a thrust of his elbow.

"What's the big picture here?" Woody asked Russ, watching Graham go down the hall to his room.

"There's been a raid."

"Who? What? Why?"

"Graham said he was raiding a lovenest."

"How many lovebirds did he find nesting in it?"

"I don't know and Connie's not talking."

"It takes more than one to make a nest," Woody said. "Where's the preacher?"

"Aimee say's he's off somewhere thinking."

"I knew I was going to get a song out of this and now it's coming on strong."

Katie pushed Russ down the hall toward their room.

"You can call it a lovenest if you want to," Katie was saying in her whiny, thin voice, "but I know different. Connie Mangrum is a contemptible loose thing. She's not a decent woman. She's nothing but a common harlot. I know all about her—most people do. She started her sinful life right here in Augusta four years ago and her mother is to blame for it. She wanted to go away then and her mother made her stay at home. If she'd left soon enough and got away from her mother, she could've been a respectable person somewhere instead of what she is now. I don't mind saying that about her even if she is your niece. I could tell what she is the minute she set foot in this house today—and exposing her nakedness in that dress she was wearing half-on and half-off. It's a disgrace for a decent woman like me to have to be around her. And the shame of it is that she lured a preacher to her room for what she is. That poor Pastor Purdy will never be the same again."

When Velma and Woody got to their room, he was humming a new tune and slowly stroking his guitar.

"Baby, what do you think?" he said to Velma. "I'll bet your sister gave the preacher a rumble-rumble he won't forget before he's ninety-nine years old. I could picture the treat she was going to give him while she was making eyes and toss-tossing her big titties at him at suppertime. I wish I could've been around to watch her style when she had him up here in her room. She's the kind who doesn't have to carry a tape measure to find out what she wants to know. You could blindfold her and tie her hands behind her back and whirl her around a dozen times and I bet she'd still figure out how much his tool would stretch before she ever saw it in the open. Baby, it sure makes me proud to be married to her sister. You're the best favor of my life."

"Are you going to make up a song about that, Woody?" Velma asked. "Please do. I want to hear it."

"It's coming on strong, baby. How did you know?"

"I can hear a tune for it the way you're getting those notes," she said as she listened. "Keep it up, Woody. Don't stop now. Let's go with it."

Woody sat down on the bed and, tapping the beat with his foot, stroked the guitar strings while Velma finished undressing as she hummed the tune he was playing.

"You picture it good, baby," he told her approvingly. "You've got the swing of it good-good. Now I know it's the real right tune. The next thing, we'll work out the right lyrics to go with it. Baby, we're going to make it so we'll take the town. Let's hear you hum it again. Give it that good-good swing of yours. With you singing it and me playing it, we're going to make Connie famous for her magic tape measure wherever the big sound goes."

Chapter 9

During the few hours Raley was in his room, after coming back into the house when all the lights had been turned off, he slept very little, and soon after dawn he woke up with a violent jerking of his body. The early morning sensation was stronger and more intense than he had ever felt it before, and as he kicked the sheet away, he was startled to see that he had taken off all his underwear before going to bed. By then he was so wide-awake that he knew he could not go back to sleep.

He had been dreaming that he came back into the house after Graham had gone to sleep and that he was alone with Connie again. Now that he was awake, he realized that it had only been a dream and his mind began racing with thoughts about what had actually happened in her room before he had to leave through the window.

Sitting on the edge of the bed, holding both hands squeezed between his legs, he stared at the wall between the two rooms as though he could actually see Connie just as she had been the night before. After a while he could see himself going into her room again and, with no embarrassment at all at being naked this time, boldly putting his arms around her and kissing her.

There was a sudden noisy roar from the big bulldozer on the other side of Mangrum Road as it was started on the day's work of scraping and terracing the ground for the new brick houses. As if it had been Graham shouting and pounding on the door, Raley got to his feet with a violent trembling and put on his clothes as quickly as he could.

Walking unsteadily, his hand still shaking nervously, Raley left the room and went downstairs to breakfast.

While serving him fried potatoes, grits, and fatback sausage, Martha asked Raley to tell her about the particular kind of religion he preached in his new church.

Annoyed to be questioned at a time like that, he did not even look up from his plate. All he wanted to think about then was being alone with Connie again. He had never before experienced the sensation of being in love and feeling so utterly miserable at the same time. All he knew about the strange feeling was that he had a longing to give Connie a present and that he had to get something for her.

Still ignoring Martha's first question, he hoped she would go away and leave him alone.

"Well, Pastor Purdy, do you do foot-washing at your church?" she asked persistently.

Continuing to eat, he shook his head.

"Then do you use a little bottle of some kind of oil and put a dab of it on the forehead of the true believers?"

"No. Some of the other religions dab oil and sprinkle water, but my religion is different."

"Then I reckon the most you do of in your church is preaching and praying."

Raley looked up and nodded. "I preach and pray like Billy Graham does. I listened to him on the radio and learned how. We both do it the same way now. You can't hardly tell the difference between us."

"Well, do you mostly preach and pray for something or against something?"

"Both. But against something is best. That makes people sit up and listen better."

"You don't want to tell much about your own particular kind of religion, do you, Pastor Purdy?"

"I'm in a big hurry now. I don't have time."

"But maybe you could explain just one thing. Does your kind of religion have a church for the colored to go to? I'd like to find out about that."

"The Supreme Being Missionary church is for the white people. The dark people have to look out for themselves about their religion just like they have to do about everything else they want."

Martha looked down at him in silence for a moment.

"I know that's no lie," she said sharply as she walked out of the room, closing the door with a loud slam.

As soon as he finished eating, Raley left the dining room and walked through the hall to the front yard. The big yellow bulldozer was working closer to the house that morning than it had ever done before, and making enough noise to wake everybody up, but nobody else had come downstairs yet.

Stopping before he got to his sag-sided automobile in the driveway, Raley reached into his pocket and carefully counted his money. As soon as he saw how little he had, he realized that it was not enough to buy something for Connie and he tried to think what he could do about getting some more money right away.

It was Friday and it would be two more days before he could pass the collection basket at the church for the Sunday offering. That was longer than he could wait to give Connie a present, and, more than that, he knew the contributions of twelve or fourteen people would not amount to enough to buy the kind of present he wanted for her. (*I've seen these preaching evangelists come down this way from the Tennessee mountains all my life and they all look and act the same. And one is just as poor-mouth and dumb-head and stiff-prick as the next one. I haven't seen one yet who went through the sixth grade, but—God Almighty—how they can preach any kind of religion and stir up the women and beg for the money. Well, if they're going to make a living, I guess that's the only thing they can do to get by, but I've seen some of them go moonlighting at any kind of job they can get when the church collections don't amount to enough. I'll give them credit for going out and working like that even if I don't want nothing to do with their kind of religion. Presbyterian is good enough for me—or I'd take my wife's Lutheran if I had to change.*) Raley had never before bought a gift for a girl and he wondered what he could get that Connie would want. However, he remembered looking at store-window displays on Broad Street and seeing gift-wrapped boxes and other things for sale that were priced at only a few dollars.

What Raley decided to do then was to get his car started so he could drive to the church on Reynolds Street. It had been his habit since renting the building to sweep the floor of the church on Friday to get it ready for the Sunday services, and he hoped that while he was sweeping and dusting he would think of a way to get the money he needed.

However, just as it had done the day before when he tried to start his car after running into the tree, the engine merely

90

sputtered weakly several times before quitting completely. He knew then that he would have to work on the engine before the car would run again. He got his faded bibbed overalls from the back seat and put them on to keep from getting grease on his shirt and pants, then took out the tool box to go to work.

Raley spent nearly two hours scraping the carbon from the valves and cleaning the spark plugs and then adjusting the ignition timer to keep the engine from backfiring. After that he crawled under the car to tighten the bolts on the crankcase to stop all the oil from dripping to the ground.

He was still tightening the bolts under the car when Aimee and Graham came from the house on the way to their automobile in the driveway. Hoping to keep Graham from knowing he was there, he put down the wrench so he would not make any sound under his car. When Aimee saw his long legs sticking out, however, she bent over as far as she could and called to him.

"Pastor Purdy, are you all right under there?" she asked with concern. "Is anything wrong with you? I've been looking all over the house for you and couldn't find you anywhere. Martha said you ate your breakfast a while ago but didn't know what became of you after that. I even went to Connie's room to look for you, but she said she hadn't seen you since last night. You don't know how worried I've been. Are you sure you feel all right, Pastor Purdy?"

"I'm just under here fixing my car, Mrs. Mangrum," he answered. He could see Graham standing not far away and he decided to stay where he was and not go anywhere near Graham. In order to protect himself even more, realizing that Graham might stomp him, he drew his feet all the way under the car. "I'll have it running good again in a little while, Mrs. Mangrum. All it needs is a little fixing."

"Well, Graham's going to drive me to the downtown stores

and I'm going to get myself a comfortable pair of shoes like I've been needing for a long time and couldn't afford till now that I've got some money that Cato Boykin handed me yesterday. Don't you want to ride downtown with us, Pastor Purdy?"

"I can't do that now, Mrs. Mangrum."

"It'd sure make me feel proud to be seen walking up and down Broad Street with you."

"But I've got to stay right here till I finish fixing my car, Mrs. Mangrum. I can't stop now."

"I might just treat you to a pair of shoes for yourself, Pastor Purdy. I've got the money for it."

Raley remained silent, thinking about the amount of money that would be spent for a pair of shoes for him.

"Well, all right then," he heard Aimee say, "I'll just have to go and leave you. But don't you worry about all that commotion upstairs last night. It wasn't your fault and Graham's sorry about it now and everything's going to be nice and friendly. Graham promised me."

Nothing more was said and he waited under the car until he saw Aimee and Graham leave the driveway. Then he crawled out and brushed the dirt from his greasy overalls. The engine began running smoothly as soon as he started it, and he was so pleased that he drove away without waiting to take off his overalls. He knew there was very little gasoline left in the tank and he went up Mangrum Road to Gene Infinger's filling station to buy enough to get to Reynolds Street and back.

When Raley stopped at the filling station, he counted out a dollar in nickels and dimes and handed the money to Gene. While Bunson was pumping into the tank as much gasoline as the dollar would buy, Gene counted the money a second time.

"I haven't seen you before," Gene said, looking closely at him. "You live around here?"

"I moved in Mrs. Mangrum's house last night."

"Well, I'll be Goddamned. Are you another Mangrum?"

"I'm no kin to them. I only board there."

"I'm glad you're not another one. But I didn't think you could be a Mangrum—not after you'd paid me cash in advance for the gas. How long have you been around here?"

"I came about three weeks ago."

"Do you want to make some money?"

"How?" he asked at once.

"I need somebody like you to help me out. You look hungry enough to want to do good on a job. Anybody who can keep a Goddamned old junker like that car of yours running ought to be able to work around a filling station. And you've already got your work clothes on. Have you ever done anything like this before?"

"Not exactly, but I worked at a sawmill back up in East Tennessee before I came down here."

"What did you do at that sawmill?"

"I was an engine oiler and wiper and a tool handler and things like that."

"You look like a tool handler. What's your name?"

"Raley Purdy."

Gene stepped forward and shook hands with him.

"I'm Gene Infinger. Everybody calls me Gene—but not that colored boy. I'll pay you the government minimum, Raley."

"How much is that?"

"I'll have to figure it out on a piece of paper first and then I'll show it to you. It's more than I want to pay, God damn it, but I can't help myself with the screwing government breathing down my neck like a Saturday-night hooker with the rent unpaid. They make me pay that colored boy Bunson the same way, too, just like he was white. God damn it, he's not worth it but I can't help myself."

"I sure need to make some money somehow," Raley said.

"Okay, Raley. Move your car out of sight around behind

the station where people can't see it and I'll start showing you what to do. I want you to work a part-time day for five hours and then all day Saturdays and Sundays for ten hours. You'll get one day off a week, just like they make me let Bunson do, but not Saturdays and Sundays because that's the busiest times around here. It's about eleven o'clock now and you'll get off work today at four. God damn it, Raley, I'm sure glad you came along. I need you."

"Work on Sundays?" Raley said, backing away.

"Sure. Sunday is just as busy as Saturday at this location right off the expressway. People go fishing and sporting and God knows what else on weekends and they need gas and oil to get to hell-and-gone and back. You know how it is. You can't go screwing around without gas in the tank."

"But I preach on Sundays."

"You do what? Preach? You mean that?"

Raley nodded.

"Well, I'll be Goddamned! I didn't know I was talking to a preacher. You sure didn't look like a preacher when you got here and you still don't look like one to me. What kind of preacher are you?"

"Supreme Being Missionary."

"What's that?"

"It's a new church I started on Reynolds Street about three weeks ago when I got here—"

"You started a new religion yourself?"

Raley nodded. "It's the kind Billy Graham talks about on the radio every Sunday. That's why I did it. I want to be like Billy Graham."

"I thought I'd heard of all the kinds of religion," Gene said, "but that's a brand-new one to me. I've listened to Billy Graham, but I thought he was just selling himself along with God. Anyhow, that don't make a bit of difference now. If you're going to be preaching on Sundays, you won't do me no

94

good at all. I need a backslider for this job more than I do a preacher. My wife makes me take her to her Baptist church on Sunday mornings and that's all of two or three hours when you add up all the time it takes for washing your ass and dressing up in clothes that don't look like yourself. I can't afford to close down my filling station all that time and lose that much business. That's why I need a white man here on the job to tell Bunson what to do while I'm gone Sunday mornings."

"But I need the job," Raley said urgently. "I'll close up the church for a while and then open it up again some other time. I need the pay real bad right now."

"You'll do what?"

"I'll close it up for a while."

"You can close up a church—just like that?"

"It's all right for me to do it."

"I didn't think Billy Graham would want a church shut down. That don't sound like him."

"I'll pray about it and make it all right."

"But what about the members?"

"I don't have enough members so far to keep it going good, anyhow. It won't hurt nothing to close it down a little while. I've got to make some money some other way. And if I start working for you right now, can I draw a little pay at quitting time? I sure would appreciate it if you'd help me out like that. I've got a special reason for it."

"You must have a hell of a special reason if you'll shut down a church so you can work at a filling station. You make me feel like a Goddamned heathen, letting you do a thing like that. I know what my wife would say if she found out about it."

Gene leaned against a gasoline pump and looked curiously at Raley's tall thin body and bushy black hair. He was still uncertain about what to do when he spoke again.

"God damn it, you sure have got me baffled," he said to Raley. "I didn't know what I was getting into when I offered you the job and I still don't know. But, God damn, I don't like to offer a man a job and then turn around and take it away from him for no good reason. And how'll I know if you'll come back to work again after today if I let you have some money against your pay?"

"Oh, I'll promise to keep on working for you. And you can believe me because I'm a preacher."

"Well," Gene said, finally making up his mind, "if I can't believe a preacher, I don't know nobody else I could believe. And you look hungry enough to want to keep on working. I'll let you have a little money against your pay at quitting time at four o'clock so you can get something to eat or whatever it is you want money for. That's it. You go ahead and start work, Raley."

Gene sent Bunson to the shed for a push-broom.

"The first thing I want you to do," Gene told Raley when Bunson came back with the broom, "is to sweep all the trash off this concrete apron around the filling station nice and clean and make it look good to the customers. People don't like to drive up and spend their money at a messy-looking gas station. Then when you finish that, I want you to put my car on the rack and give it a damn good wash job so it'll look good when I have to drive my wife to church Sunday. Maybe in a day or two I'll put you to pumping gas and cleaning windshields and things like that. I don't expect you to learn every damn thing the first day on the job. It'd take anybody a little while to learn to run the business the way I want it done. But you just do like I tell you and you'll catch on in no time at all. And I'll try to watch my talk around here while you're on the job. But, God damn it, it ain't going to be easy for me even if you are a preacher."

Chapter 10

It was a little after four o'clock in the afternoon when Gene Infinger called Raley to the office and handed him four limp one-dollar bills. Raley had worked five hours since starting at eleven that morning without stopping to eat or rest. Having had nothing to eat since breakfast, by then he felt light-headed and weak in the knees, but he had no thought of spending any of the four dollars for something to eat.

"Wait a minute, Raley," Gene said as he turned to leave. "I'm curious about something. Are you one of the people who paint the religious signs and put them up along the roads? The kind that say Christ is coming and get ready for eternity and don't let the devil fool you and things like that?"

"No. Those people don't have the true religion. They don't

97

even have churches to go to and never hear preaching and praying. All they do is paint signs and nail them up. They save money that way by not paying a preacher and keeping up a church. But God wants people to listen to preaching and praying the way me and Billy Graham do it and pay in money for it. That's why God says we're the chosen people."

Gene nodded. "I see. I didn't know that about getting chosen. I'm glad you came along so I could learn it."

"I'm in a hurry now," Raley said, backing away, "but I'll pray for you when I come to work tomorrow and see to it that you get chosen too."

"No you won't! I'll be Goddamned if you'll do that on working time that I'm paying you for!"

Putting the four dollars into an inside pocket and promising Gene to come back to work the next day, Raley took off his overalls and threw them on the back seat of his car. Then he drove to the expressway and hurried eastward toward Reynolds Street at the levee.

When he got to the storefront church, he found a pencil and a clean sheet of paper in the litter that had accumulated on the back seat of the car. Then he began lettering a sign to put on the church door to notify the members that there would be no more religious services for a while and that he would put up another sign when preaching was to start again. He hung the notice on a nail on the door and hurried back to his car to drive the few blocks to the stores on Broad Street.

While working at the filling station during the afternoon, Raley had tried to think of what kind of present he could get for Connie. He knew it would have to be something that cost no more than four dollars, as well as something that was a suitable gift for a pretty girl like Connie. While driving to Reynolds Street and lettering the notice for the church door, he had tried to remember what he had seen in the store windows that he could buy. He had thought of jewelry, radios, rugs, handbags, foot stools, sofa pillows, lamp shades, framed pictures, and kitchen utensils, but he decided that such things either would be unsuitable or would cost too much money.

After finding a parking place on Broad Street in front of some of the stores, he got out of the car and began to walk slowly along the block and look at the window displays. It was almost five o'clock by then and the sidewalk was crowded with late-afternoon shoppers. Besides being anxious to take Connie a present as soon as he could, he was afraid the stores would close for the night before he could find something to buy.

Raley had seen several stores that had elaborate window displays of underwear for women and he had hurried past each one as quickly as he could with only a sidelong glance at the garments. Other than shops selling shoes and jewelry and men's clothing, nearly all the others in the block displayed women's stockings and underwear and he soon began to worry more than ever about finding a suitable present.

Just before reaching the end of the block, though, he saw a store window with a startling array of garter belts and split-hip panties and lacy brassieres in all styles and colors. Stopping for a moment, and then cautiously going closer, he was soon fascinated by the sight of the scanty garments on the life-size mannequins. The mannequins looked as if they would become real live women any moment and he was too spellbound to think of walking away.

Putting his hand into his pocket, Raley clutched the limp money to make sure it was still there. Some of the garments were priced low enough to buy with the money he had and he knew right away that he wanted to get one of them for Connie. By then, all the mannequins looked exactly like Connie and he could see their eyes looking at him enticingly just as he remembered hers doing when he went into her room.

Of all the garments on the mannequins, the one he decided he wanted to take to Connie was a black lace brassiere with two large round openings for her breasts to be seen bare through. He had preached several times against women wearing short skirts and low-necked dresses, but he had never known before that they wore garments with large holes in them so their breasts would purposely be uncovered. He thought for a moment about preaching against that, but quickly put it out of his mind. As it was, the longer he stared at the revealing brassiere, the more eager he became to see Connie put it on and take it off.

He walked as far as the doorway of the store and then found he could go no farther. All the clerks and customers were women and there was not a man among them. That was when a feverish feeling of fright came over him and he knew he could never go inside and say he wanted to buy something that was on display in the window. More than that, he realized then that he would have to point at what he wanted to buy and be even more embarrassed.

Raley turned around and walked away with his long stride as quickly as he could. (*I know him. He came to my house a couple of weeks ago asking for money for his church. I felt sort of sorry for him and I gave him fifty cents and told him to sit down and talk a while. That's how I found out how he came to be a preacher. He said his father was a moonshiner up there in the Tennessee mountains and one of his sisters had a baby that belonged to his own daddy. His mother was very religious, though, and she made him promise to get out and preach against liquor and fornication. When he left home, his mother gave him her Bible and his daddy gave him a six-shooter pistol. He said they were the only two things he had in the world except his clothes and a seventy-five-dollar car he bought with his sawmill wages. I felt just as sorry for him when he left as I did at the start and that's why I've gone to his church on Reynolds Street a couple of times to hear him preach and put a little money in the collection.*) As he hurried away from the store, Raley looked straight ahead, fearful that some of the people on the crowded sidewalk were members of his church and had seen him looking at a store window with such a bold display of women's underwear.

At the end of the block, he had to stop to wait for the traffic light to change. When he looked around cautiously to see if anybody on the street recognized him, he found that he was standing in front of a drugstore that had an elaborate window display of boxes of candy. Grateful to see something he could buy without embarrassment, and unworried then about being recognized by one of his members, he went inside and bought the largest box of chocolate candy he could get for four dollars. The big box was wrapped in shiny green paper with a bright red ribbon around it.

With the box of candy placed close beside him on the front seat of the car so he could reach down and touch it now and then, he left Broad Street and went directly to the expressway to drive to Mangrum Road. It was a cloudless day, mildly warm and still about an hour before sunset. He whistled all the way to the Mangrum mansion, and then when he got there, he drove carefully into the driveway so he would not run into one of the big oak trees again.

Raley could see some of the Mangrums sitting on the veranda as he switched off the engine, and he decided to wait in the automobile for a while before going to the house to give Connie the present. He wanted to be alone with Connie when he gave her the candy and he hoped everybody would soon leave the veranda and go back into the house.

As soon as the noisy engine had stopped running, Raley could hear loud voices. He listened closely to hear if the Mangrums were talking about his being in Connie's room and jumping out the window to the porch roof.

101

There were two suitcases and several large bundles of clothing at the top of the veranda steps and Katie was standing there pointing her finger at Aimee. Velma and Woody were sitting on the settee, now far away, and Russ was standing behind Katie. Raley was relieved when he did not see Graham anywhere.

"You took the last rug out of my room today and put it on the floor in that Pastor Purdy's room, Aimee Mangrum," Katie was saying angrily. "You did that mean thing so I'd have to put my bare feet on the cold floor when I get out of bed in the morning."

Raley leaned as far out the window of his car as he could in order to be able to hear better.

"When you did that sneaky mean thing, that's what decided me to get out of this house. You wanted me to get splinters in my toes on that splintery floor, didn't you? Well, I wouldn't stay in this house now another night even if you got down on your knees and begged me to. If you begged me right now, I'd laugh in your face. I'm going to live with my own true relatives. They're decent people. They're nothing like you Mangrums. You've been sneaking in my room when I wasn't there and taking furniture and things away piece by piece for the past eight years and that proves how much meanness you've got in you."

Aimee wiped tears from her face with both hands.

"I didn't mean no harm at all, Katie."

"I won't listen to your excuses."

"But I'm so sincere about it."

"Don't you try to stop me while I'm telling you how mean you are, Aimee Mangrum. You're always talking about how sorry you are for people and then you turn right around and do nasty mean things to me behind my back. You're a two-faced mean old thing. Only yesterday you took my sewing table out of my room, too. That's why I'm leaving this house and moving in with my own relatives who'll treat me decent. They'll be glad to have me living with them and won't never treat me like you do."

"I'll put the rug back, Katie," she said tearfully. "I only did it because I felt sorry for Pastor Purdy being barefooted on the splintery floor and I'll find another rug for him. And you can have your table back, too. I couldn't stand it if you and Russell left me. The house would be too big and empty without you and him after being used to you all this time. Ever since I buried Ralph ten years ago it wrings my heart when somebody leaves me like James and Connie did. Please don't go, Katie. I couldn't be more sincere. I've got to have all my kinfolks right here in the house with me for my peace of mind and to keep me from suffering. I give you my promise, Katie. You can have everything back I ever took out of your room."

Aimee reached out and tried to put her hand on Katie's arm. Katie moved backward with a jerk of her thin body.

"You can't bribe me talking like that. And I don't believe a word you say, anyhow. You'll sneak things out of my room again just like you've always done. I know all about your sneaky ways. You've treated me mean ever since I married Russell and moved in. I married him and put up with you this long to be here to get the rightful share of all the property that's due him. I wouldn't have married him if I'd known you'd keep me and him poor like you do. You won't share it with him because you don't want me to get any benefit from it."

"I try to manage the best I can, Katie. A widow has a hard time managing things."

"You manage to put everything in your own pocketbook. Russell is as much his father's son as Ralph Mangrum ever was and he ought to have had half of everything a long time ago. You've been selling off the land all this time till there's hardly nothing left to divide up. When you get money like that, you put it all in your own pocket. Just look at all that land over there across the road that you sold off and where they're building all those fine houses. Half of that rightfully belonged to Russell and you sneaked around and sold it off without giving him a penny of the money you got for it. It's a disgrace the way you treat Russell and me about money."

Aimee lifted the hem of her skirt and dried some of the tears on her face.

"And now you've gone and moved that Pastor Purdy in the house," Katie said bitterly. "The Lord knows what you'll be taking away from Russell now and giving him—a somebody who doesn't even have a religion anybody ever heard of before. A good sanctified Methodist like you used to be wouldn't do an unchristian thing like that."

"It's my duty to help Pastor Purdy," Aimee protested. "I feel sorry for him just like I do for my real kinfolks and I want to provide meals and a place to live for everybody. That's why I have to get money somehow to do that."

"You've got your eye on marrying him, that's what! A woman your age contriving to marry a man only half as old as you are! You ought to hang your head in shame! Just because he's handsome, you overlook that he can barely read and write! And you say you provide meals! Well, I'll tell you something about the meals you provide. I've been constipated and making gas ever since I moved in here and had to eat the kind of meals you provide. I have to dose myself with medicine all the time because of that. You ask Dr. Price. He knows all about it. He told me the kind of medicine I'd have to take all the time to relieve myself. You ought to be ashamed of yourself for making me like that. You ask anybody else who eats here and they'll tell you the same things about the meals."

"Don't you dare criticize Martha Washington for that," Aimee said sharply. "I won't stand for it. She's the best cook

104

in the whole city of Augusta besides being honest and faithful like she is. Now you take that back about her!"

"I'm not blaming Martha Washington for nothing. She can't help it. Martha Washington has to cook the awful food you go out and buy. But I bet she does most of her eating at her own house."

Katie turned and looked at Velma and Woody sitting together on the settee.

"If you won't believe me, ask Woody Woodruff. He's an outsider who moved in here. And you've heard him complain plenty of times about all the greasy fatback sausage everybody has to eat. Go on and ask him—if you're not scared to hear what he says."

"Don't you picture me," Woody said with an emphatic shaking of his head that wagged his beard. "I'll compose a folksong about your constipation and gas, but I'm sure not going to talk myself out of a place to sleep and eat—no matter how much grease I have to squeeze out of the sausage. I've got it too good here in Miss Mamma Aimee's house to do a fool thing like that."

Taking several steps backward, Aimee regarded Katie with an angry flush on her face. No longer were there any tears in her eyes.

"You've been talking mean about me all this time," she began, "and now it's my turn to tell you what I've got against you. I never did think much of you from the day you somehow tricked Russell to marry you because you thought you'd be getting some Mangrum money, but I've put up with you for his sake. He's a real Mangrum and I felt sorry for him getting tricked into marrying an outsider like you. If it wasn't for him, I wouldn't have nothing to do with somebody with your peculiar family name."

"Don't you dare run down my family!" Katie said.

"You be quiet while I'm talking. And I'm only getting

started, too. Your tricky scheming didn't fool me—trying to get some Mangrum money. And another thing you married Russell for was so you could change your name because you're ashamed of it and wanted to take on our aristocratic Mangrum name. The first time I heard somebody mention the Snoddyhouse family, I said to myself, uh-huh, that's a Yankee name if I ever heard one. Snoddyhouse! I snicker every time I hear it!"

"The Snoddyhouse family is just as good as yours!"

"If it's so good, why did you marry outside it?"

"Because in my family we're too decent to marry first cousins like you did. We have high ideals."

"You've got no right to talk about my late husband Ralph now that he's dead and gone."

"I don't have to mention him by name when there are certain other Mangrums I could mention for what I'm talking about. They show what happens when first cousins marry."

"You shut your mouth, Katie Snoddyhouse! I won't stand hearing you talk like that. I know who you mean, but Graham is different than other people. Now, you go on and move in with your Snoddyhouse relatives and I'll be glad to see you leave and stay there. But I want Russell to stay here. He's a Mangrum and the only brother-in-law I've got and I don't want him to leave."

"Russell is my husband and Russell will do exactly what I tell him to do."

Russ, with a meek turning of his head, fixed his gaze upon something he found interesting in the front yard.

"You don't know it, Katie Snoddyhouse," Aimee said with a pleased expression on her round pink face, "but I told Cato Boykin I want him to get all the money he can for all the Mangrum property that's left and he's busy about doing it right now this minute. When the money comes in, I'm going

106

to be rolling in wealth and I'm going to set some of it aside for Russell for his share. The only thing I could be sorry about—if I wanted to—and I don't—is that you're leaving and moving in with your own relatives and won't never get a bit of benefit from it."

Katie glanced quickly across the veranda at Russ. He had turned around when he heard Aimee mention his name.

"Well," Katie said to Aimee with a pleasant smile, "well, that's different. I didn't know about that. Did you hear what she said, Russell?"

Before he could say anything, Katie began talking excitedly.

"That makes me think a lot different about leaving now. I'm afraid I let myself get too upset about little unimportant things and outspoke myself when I didn't really mean it. I want to do what's best for Russell for his sake. I've always felt that way about Russell all these years we've been married. That's why I don't want to take him away now. He belongs here at the family place."

Reaching down and picking up one of the bundles, Katie called to Russ and told him to carry the suitcases and all the other bundles back upstairs to their room. Russ, frowning defiantly, hesitated for several moments and made no move to do as he had been told. Then, when Katie motioned to him with a commanding sweep of her arm, he grunted with disappointment and picked up the suitcases. She was the first to leave.

"I could've stayed and let her go," he said, cautiously lowering his voice. "I wish she hadn't changed her mind about that."

Aimee was too far away then to hear what Russ was saying as he continued talking to himself when he left the veranda. She sat down in one of the chairs and made herself comfortable. After that, she closed her eyes with a contented sigh.

A taxicab came into the driveway, stopping beside Raley's car, and the driver immediately sounded three short beeps with the horn. Then he leaned back in the seat with a friendly wave of his hand to Raley.

Curious to know why a taxicab would be coming to the Mangrum house, Raley called to the grinning round-faced driver. He was not able to hear what Raley was saying and he turned off the noisy crackling of the taxi's radio.

"How's that again, fellow?" the driver asked.

"Who are you?"

"Me? Everybody knows me. I'm Buster."

"What did you come here for?"

"To pick up a passenger, fellow."

"Who?"

"She's that good-looking Mangrum girl I brought out here yesterday from the bus station. The classy blonde. The one with all the goodies. I used to know her before she left town a couple of years ago. Boy! Is she classy now!"

"You mean—Connie—"

"That's right. You know her?"

Raley glanced quickly at the doorway of the house and then looked at the taxi driver again.

"Where's Connie—where's she going?"

"Well, now, fellow, you're getting pretty personal, ain't you? I don't know who the hell you are and I don't go around telling strangers everything I know. Some things are not everybody's God damn business. Who the hell are you, anyhow?"

"I'm Pastor Purdy and I—"

"A preacher? What kind of preacher?"

"Supreme Being Missionary."

"Never heard of it. But if you're a real preacher, I know it's none of your business."

"But I want her to stay here."

108

"You do? Then why didn't you make a date with her before somebody else did? Now you'll have to get in line and wait your turn."

"Did somebody else—make a date—"

"What the hell, fellow. That's the way it is."

"But not Connie—I don't want Connie to—"

Connie came out of the house and, not looking at anybody on the veranda, ran down the walkway to the taxi. She was wearing her thin black dress and carrying a jacket and a hand-bag that was as large as a shopping bag. When she saw Raley, she quickly got into the taxi and closed the door. The driver started the engine at once and began backing out of the driveway.

Clutching the big box of candy, Raley got out of his car and watched the taxi moving away.

"Connie—wait a minute!" he called desperately. "Where are you going off to? Don't go away! I've got something to give you! It's a present for you!"

He ran to the end of the driveway, frantically waving for her to come back. The taxi driver beeped the horn three times and went up Mangrum Road toward the expressway. Just before the taxi went out of sight, Raley thought he saw Connie looking back at him through the rear window.

The only sound Raley could hear after that was a doleful song Woody Woodruff was singing about a night-time girl who didn't even wait for the sun to go down.

Chapter 11

After having been away all night, Connie came home in Buster's taxi shortly after eight o'clock the next morning. She went straight to her room and slept all day.

It was late when Raley Purdy left Gene Infinger's filling station that Saturday afternoon after a full day's work, and he had hurried to the Mangrum house to give Connie the box of candy.

Connie had just got out of bed and had not finished dressing when Raley knocked on her door and told her who he was.

Holding the big box of candy, which had been hidden under his bed while he was at work, he waited expectantly for Connie to open the door so he could give her the present.

On his way into the house, he had walked past Graham on the veranda without a word being spoken, and he hoped Graham would not come upstairs before he could get into Connie's room and be out of sight.

As he stood there anxiously waiting for Connie to open the door, he hoped the reason for her taking so long to let him into her room was because she was undressing for him. After dreaming about her for two nights and thinking about her all day while he was working, all he could think about now was her having been naked the first time and how much he wanted to see her like that again.

When he could no longer stand still, he began walking back and forth in front of the door and wondering if every man in love felt as he did about wanting to give a present.

Hearing somebody come into the downstairs hall from the veranda, he hurriedly knocked on Connie's door again.

"Stop that, Raley," she called to him in a scolding manner. "Don't be in such a big hurry. I'm not ready yet. And I don't like to be rushed. Go on to your room and wait for me. Find something to do till I get there—play with yourself. I'll be there in a little while."

Eagerly obeying her command and feeling elated that she had spoken to him, Raley went to his room and sat down on the bed to wait. He had left the door partly open, just as she had done the night he went into her room, and he waited nervously on the edge of the bed for the first sight of her at the doorway.

After silently repeating the exact words Connie had spoken when she promised to come to his room, he then began to wonder if she would be undressed when she got there or if she would be wearing the kind of underclothes he had seen on the store-window mannequins.

The whole house was quiet and he could not even hear a sound in the adjoining room. Tensely gripping the box of candy, Raley stared at the wall and tried to think of what Connie was doing that took so much time. He could imagine that she was undressing and combing her hair and looking at herself in the mirror, but he could not think of anything else she could be doing that would take her so long to get ready to come to his room.

It was after six o'clock and he had been waiting almost half an hour when Connie pushed the door all the way open and walked into the room. He was so surprised to see her fully dressed that he could not say a word as she came to the foot of the bed and looked down at him. She was wearing a pale-green dress that was made of material so sheer that it was almost transparent and it fitted even lower over her breasts than her revealing thin black dress. Seeing her like that instantly reminded him of the life-size mannequins, and he wondered if her underclothing was as scanty as the garments he had seen on display. Connie's bright blonde hair had been carefully combed and she was carrying her jacket and the same large purse that resembled a shopping bag.

Raley slowly got to his feet.

"Well, here I am," she said, smiling slightly. "I didn't keep you waiting too long, did I?"

"But I didn't know you'd be all dressed up like that—what I thought was—"

"Do you really like my dress, Raley?" Pleased, she turned slowly around for him to see it completely. "It's not very new, but it's one of my favorites. And you really like it? You think it's becoming?"

He nodded reluctantly.

"Well, what did you want to see me about?" she asked casually.

"Here," he said, thrusting the box of candy at her.

"What is it?"

"It's a present for you from me. It's the same present I

112

bought to give you last night. But you went off in that taxi before I could give it to you. It's candy. I got it at a drugstore downtown yesterday. It's four dollars' worth."

"That's very nice of you, Raley," she told him, smiling briefly again. "Thank you very much. I hadn't expected a present from you, but I always like to get presents from men. It gives me such a good feeling to know that somebody admires me enough to want to give me something. Thank you, Raley, for thinking of me like that."

"That's why I did it—I wanted to give you a present because—"

He stopped and stared at her blankly.

"Because?" She placed the jacket and large purse on the bed. "Because what?"

His lips were trembling nervously. "Like the other night—that's why—I love you—that's what I mean!"

She looked down at the brightly wrapped box of candy.

"What makes you think you love me?"

"I don't know—but I feel that way about you."

Now that he had been able to say it the first time, he wanted to tell her over and over that he loved her.

"I want to be where you are all the time and give you presents. I've got to love you—I can't help it—that's why I love you. I've felt like that ever since I was in your room the other night—and what you did. I can't think about nothing else. I want you some more—I'll do anything if you'll—"

"Wait a minute, Raley," she spoke up severely. "Listen to me. I'm going to tell you something before you say anything more like that. If you don't know it already, listen to it now. I'm going to give it to you straight. Any girl can get a man's fever up the way I did if she wants to. Any time, any place. It's always easy to get a man worked up like that. But nobody has to be in love every time for it. I wasn't then and I'm not now, so stop eating your heart out. I was just curious

113

about you the other night. I wanted to find out how you'd act with your fever up. And I got my thrill."

"But Connie—I love you—"

"It sounds nice to hear you keep on saying that, Raley, but it means nothing to me." She turned her head when she saw the appealing expression on his face and it was several moments before she could look at him again. "If you listen to me, you'll stop where you are before it hurts too much. I've been in love. I know all about it. You mustn't let yourself keep on thinking you're going to be in love with me just because we had a down-the-middle date. It didn't mean a damn thing after it was all over. You don't know anything about the way I really am and it'd hurt you to find out. I'm not for you. I'm not like you think I am. I date a lot of men. Be smart, Raley. Take my word for it. Somebody else would be better for you. Think of all the pretty young girls just waiting to be pushed in a corner by a handsome man. They'll get your fever up. They'll go down the middle with you. I didn't waste any time, did I? I knew you weren't a castrated monk or something and all I wanted was to find out how you'd act with your fever up. I'd never had a date with a preacher before, and I didn't know if you'd be a virgin or what, but one time was all I wanted. And I had it. Now, get yourself another girl, Raley."

"But, Connie, I love you. I don't want anybody else."

"No, Raley, no," she said, smiling sympathetically. "Don't keep on saying that. I'm not for you. Stop beating yourself. I'm glad you feel like that about me, but I keep on telling you that's all. Don't pull the zipper on your pants around me. If you want to get married, find the marrying kind. Jesus Christ! You ought to know by now I'm not the kind to marry a preacher."

"Connie, I'll do anything you want me to," he pleaded. "I'll quit preaching—I'll give up my religion—I'll—"

114

"You poor bastard." She stepped backward, biting her lip momentarily, and regarded him with a pitying expression. "You really do talk like you never had a girl get your fever up before like I did. If you keep on talking that way, you'll make me feel sorry for you and I don't want to. I'm not like Mamma. I don't want to feel sorry for anybody—except for myself sometimes."

Hesitating for a moment after drawing in her breath, Connie suddenly ran to him and put her arms around his neck. She pressed all the softness of her breasts and thighs against the hardness of his lean body and then kissed him for a long time with all the fullness of her mouth. The strength was sucked from him until his arms felt weak and useless.

There were tears in her eyes when she left him and went toward the door.

"Wait, Connie!" he called desperately. "Where are you going? Don't leave me now!"

She stopped, brushing the tears away, and looked back at him.

"Connie, I want you to stay here—like it was the other time."

She laughed. "One more time, huh?"

Raley nodded eagerly.

"You poor fevered-up bastard. I bet you'd even get down on your knees and pray for it, wouldn't you? You must have a real big jack on."

"Connie, I'll do anything—"

"Forget it, Raley," she told him in an irritated tone as her smile vanished. Her manner was harsh and ruthless. "Cool it off. I told you I had my thrill the first time and got what I wanted. And that first time was amateur night. The next time would be pro night and it'd cost you a hell of a lot more than a cheap box of drugstore candy."

"You're not going to do that again—this time—"

"You dumb bastard! I keep on telling you I had my thrill. And it won't do you any good to keep on begging. Take your jack downtown and pick up a girl and get it done. And try to pay for it with that."

She tossed the box of candy on the bed and got her jacket and the big handbag.

"Don't you want to open the box and eat some of the candy?" Raley asked.

"If I ate it, I'd lose my girlish figure. My dates wouldn't like me then. They don't want fat to get in the way. You wouldn't want fat on me, either, would you, Raley?"

"But I bought it for you—"

"Give it to Velma—or to Mamma," she told him as she was leaving the room. "And then stay around. That'd save you a trip downtown."

Raley, unable to say anything after that, followed her along the hall as far as the stairway. Standing there helplessly, he watched Connie go down to the lower hall and then to the veranda. A few moments later the loud beeping of the taxi horn could be heard throughout the house.

He was still standing at the top of the stairway when Martha came to the lower hall from the kitchen and began ringing the big brass bell to let everybody know that supper was on the table in the dining room.

Aimee was the first to leave her room. When she saw Raley, she gripped his arm with an eager grasp and took him downstairs with her. It was the first time Aimee had seen Raley during the day and she immediately began talking about what she was going to do about going to church on Sunday. Raley had told Martha at breakfast that morning about his job at the filling station and that he would have to work all day Saturday and Sunday. Later that morning, Martha had told Aimee about it.

"It's an awful shame you had to close down your church

for a while to go to work, Pastor Purdy," Aimee was saying as they went into the dining room. "Somehow it's mighty like a sacrilege for a preacher to have to work like ordinary people. It just don't seem right. But maybe it's all for the best that you won't be preaching tomorrow and I'll tell you why in a minute. What I want to say first, though, is that if you'd told me you needed some money, I'd have given you all you wanted and you wouldn't have to work at that filling station. Cato Boykin is going to put nine hundred dollars in the bank for me Monday and then a lot more after that too. I already feel like I'm rolling in wealth."

Aimee sat down at her usual place at the table and motioned to Raley to sit beside her.

"But anyhow," she continued, spreading her fleshy buttocks comfortably on the chair, "about closing down your church for a while. I just haven't had the time yet to withdraw my membership from the Methodists and I'd feel like I was the worst of all heathen sinners on earth if I went to preaching at the Supreme Being Missionary church while I was still a Methodist. I never heard of anybody belonging to two different religions at the same time and that's why it might be the worst sin of them all. Some gossipy mean woman would tell that Methodist preacher all about it if I went to the preaching at your church and then that wife of his would be sure to nag him to preach a sermon against me. I never could stand to be preached at when I knew I'd done something bad. Anyhow, after I get my membership away from the Methodists, I'll feel more pure and holy when I go to your church, Pastor Purdy. I know that's the kind of woman you want me to be."

Katie and Russ sat down at their usual places at the table and in a few moments Velma and Woody got there. Graham, stomping his heavy shoes on the wooden floor, was the last to come in and sit down. Aimee passed the serving dishes to Raley first, while Graham glared sullenly over the table.

117

"It's a pity Connie can't be here to sit down with all the family for supper tonight," Aimee was saying. "The Mangrums always did make a great to-do about everybody sitting down to eat together at mealtime and talk. That's one of the fine Mangrum traditions—to sit at the table at supper and talk and talk and talk—and I want to pass it on to everybody when I die. Martha complains about it and says it takes up too much time and makes her get home late, but she's colored and can't appreciate traditions like we do. Anyhow, I'm glad Connie is so popular in Augusta that people want her to eat with them. I wouldn't stand in her way when she's invited to go somewhere like she was tonight. I'm proud of her going around in the social life of Augusta. The Mangrums have always been in the society set ever since I can remember. Augusta wouldn't even have any high society to boast about if it wasn't for us."

"Why does she always go off in a taxi with that same disreputable-looking man driving it?" Katie asked.

Aimee tasted some of the food on her plate and pretended not to have heard Katie's question.

"Why is it nobody ever comes for her in a private automobile in a dignified way?" Katie said, speaking out more loudly. "There're certain standards that good people live by."

Aimee continued to ignore Katie by looking around and smiling at everybody else at the table.

"I don't know what that taxi driver's name is," Katie continued, "but he's always the same man coming and going. I have my suspicions about that. If she was a daughter of mine—"

"I don't want to hear another word of that nasty kind of talk," Aimee told her, rapping a knife on the table. "There are other things to talk about and I'll thank you to do it."

"I live in this house and I have as much right to say what I please as anybody else. I'm always suspicious when I see a girl her age all dressed up in the kind of scandalous clothes she wears and looking half-undressed and riding around Augusta on the back seat of a taxi with a disreputable-looking man driving it somewhere. It's next to the most sinful thing I can think of for a girl to do."

"If what you say is next to," Woody said to Katie, taking out his comb and running it through his beard, "what's that most sinful thing you've got in mind?"

"You're always bringing up indecent things like that, Woody Woodruff, and I'll thank you not to insult me again. If Velma was the kind of girl she ought to be, she wouldn't allow you to say such awful things in my presence. That's the trouble with a lot of women these days—they don't have control over the men they marry. And if Velma had been what she ought to be in the first place, she wouldn't have married somebody like you."

Woody put his arm around Velma and hugged her. "She's my baby and the best music arranger in the business. She's going to put my combo in the top slot. Picture that, madam."

"I don't even know what you're talking about when you use that peculiar language, Woody Woodruff."

"Okay. Skip it, madam. But if I'm going to make up a song about a girl going somewhere on the back seat of a taxi, I've got to picture how sinful something is before I can compose the music and lyrics. That's why I need the comparison, madam. What is that other worst sin?"

"That's something for you to ask Connie Mangrum. She knows more about it than anybody else. Tonight's the second time she's gone off in a taxi like that. And she'll probably stay out all night again like she did the first time and then not come back till eight or nine o'clock in the morning."

Aimee rapped her knife on the table.

"I'm not going to sit here at the same table with you and listen to another shameful word you say about Connie," she told Katie with an angry raising of her voice. "You can just save yourself the trouble of opening your mouth in my presence from now on, Katie Snoddyhouse!"

"I don't care if you don't listen," Katie said with a toss of her head. "That won't keep me from saying what I want to. I married into the Mangrum family and I don't intend to keep my mouth shut about what goes on and let my good name be ruined by her awful behavior. Riding all over Augusta night and day with a disreputable-looking taxi driver taking her goodness knows where for what! The idea of coming home for a social visit—and then doing a thing like that in public!"

Aimee rapped her knife on the table again but Katie ignored her.

"I'll feel a lot easier in my soul when she goes back to Savannah where she belongs now. I've always heard that's the most sinful city in the whole country. She'll turn Augusta into the same kind of sinful place if she stays here much longer, and it won't be a decent place for people like me to live in. If she'd left home a lot sooner than she did two years ago and gone somewhere else beside Savannah, she could've made a good woman of herself. I know something about her running wild in Augusta in those days and learning her ways. And I could point my finger straight at who's to blame for it, too."

Katie got up, looking from one person to the next with a disdainful tightening of her thin lips, and then she walked out of the dining room without finishing her meal. As soon as she had gone, Russ lowered his head over his plate and ate hurriedly so he could go bowling that night and still have plenty of time for a visit on Telfair Street before getting home by midnight as Katie told him to do.

Aimee served Raley a second helping of rice custard and scraped the dish until none was left. Graham, like all the others at the table, had had only one helping from the dessert

120

dish, and when he saw there was no more custard left for him, he shoved his chair backward against the wall as hard as he could and left the room with a stomping of his heavy shoes.

"It's time for us to get going to the club, baby," Woody told Velma, pushing back his chair and motioning for her to hurry. "Let's be on the move, baby. It's payday night and I can already picture that money-money going down in my pocket."

By the time Raley had finished eating the custard and got up to leave, everyone else except Aimee had left the dining room. She sat there for a long time, wondering when she would have the best opportunity to get into Katie's room and take away another piece of furniture. She was still sitting there and thinking about it when Martha came to take the dishes away.

Chapter 12

When Martha came into the dining room, instead of stacking the dishes and picking up the knives and forks, she stood with her arms folded and waited for Aimee to look in her direction.

"What's the matter, Martha?" Aimee asked, finally turning and looking at her. "Why are you standing there like that? You always say you want to hurry and get home early at night. Go ahead and clear the table. Everybody's finished eating and left."

Martha came closer to the table then but still did not touch the dishes.

"Miss Mamma Aimee, I've got something to say to you."

"What is it? Are you going to stand there and complain about your pay again? This's no time for that. I don't want to get my stomach upset so soon after eating. I'll talk to you about it tomorrow."

"It's not about the pay now. It's too late for that."

"Then what is it?"

"Miss Mamma Aimee, it's that I've got to stop working here for you. I'm going to work for somebody else. And if you say I've got to work out the notice for two weeks, I'll have to do it but I don't want to. I want to quit right now. It's Saturday night and I want to leave and go home and not come back."

"Martha Washington—you can't do that!" Aimee protested loudly, pressing her hands against her round pink face. "What in the world are you saying! You can't walk out and leave me after all this time. You're just like one of the family to me now. I wouldn't know what in the world to do without you. I'd be helpless. It's too hard to find good servants to work for reasonable pay these days. I'd have to do my own housework. I just won't hear of you quitting. Now, you take back what you said a minute ago, and I won't hold it against you. I'll feel forgiving about it. You know how sorry I've always felt for you."

"It can't be helped now, Miss Mamma Aimee, no matter how sorry you feel for me. I've made up my mind about it and it won't be changed. I know it'll be hard on you doing all the cooking and cleaning, but it's been hard on me, too. You could get Miss Katie to help you out."

"I wouldn't dare eat a bite of food Katie Snoddyhouse had anything to do with. It'd be just like her to put rat poison in it and feed it to me."

"I forgot about that, Miss Mamma Aimee," she said with a worried clasping of her hands. "I don't blame you for not trusting Miss Katie. I heard her talking about something bad happening to you."

Aimee sat up erectly.

"What kind of something bad?"

"She wouldn't say exactly about it."

"Well, I can't think of anything worse than you walking out and leaving me high and dry. Did Katie Snoddyhouse put you up to quitting me and going to work for somebody else?"

"It wasn't her, Miss Mamma Aimee. I made up my own mind about that."

Aimee leaned back in her chair with a weary sigh and gazed unseeingly across the room as tears came to her eyes.

"This is the worst calamity that ever struck me," she sobbed. Tears began trickling down her cheeks and she made no effort to wipe them away. "I'll never find anybody else to do the work for me like you do, Martha. You've been like a black angel taking care of me all these years. We've never worked like servants ourselves in our family. The Mangrums are not like other people. Now the whole house will go to wrack and ruin without you here to cook and sweep and take care of the rooms. It's just more than I can do."

"That's the whole big trouble," Martha told her. "You bring in other people all the time to cook for and clean up after and you still don't give the rightful pay for all the work. The way it is now, though, you couldn't pay me enough to want to stay and keep on. I didn't mind Miss Connie coming home for a short visit. But when you moved Pastor Purdy in here for me to cook for and clean up his room, I just had to go out and look for another job where I'd be treated right. And if I didn't leave, you'd be just as liable to move somebody else in the house like you did him, too."

"You know how sorry I feel for Pastor Purdy, Martha. I just had to do that for him. It would've been on my conscience if I hadn't brought him here to do something for. I knew I had to do something for him ever since the first time I saw him. I'm not finished doing something for him, either."

"Maybe so, and you go right on about it, but I don't feel

124

sorry enough for him to keep on doing something for him for nothing. He may be a fine preacher for white people, but he told me he's not going to share his religion with the colored. When I hear that kind of talk, it sounds too much like the White Cross to suit me."

Aimee raised her hands to her face and wiped away some of the tears on her cheeks.

"As sure as the rising sun, Martha Washington, I know what put you up to doing this," she said with a confident nodding of her head. "Uh-huh! I know it with all my heart and soul. I can tell. You've been listening to some of those troublemaking people of your race. That's what it is. I can tell by the way you stand there and talk out of your place. Your own troublemaking people put you up to quitting just out of spite against white people. They're trying to keep colored servants from working for us so we'll suffer. It's like that disappointment club your people used to have. Only this is worse now because you want to quit for good instead of just staying away from work a day or two when you know you're needed most.

"I know what's behind all this. It's that Martin Luther King. He's always thinking up something harmful to do to white people. Somebody ought to take him aside and give him a good talking-to for the good of your race. It hurts me to see you let Martin Luther King put those kind of notions in your head. I've always felt sorry for you and you know it."

"None of that is why I made up my mind to quit, Miss Mamma Aimee. I don't have any hard feelings against you. And it wasn't somebody else's talk—it was my own thinking."

"I don't believe you. And I've got a good mind to tell the White Cross people on you."

"They can't scare me now like they used to."

Aimee was thoughtfully silent for a while.

"Martha," she said presently with an engaging smile, "Martha, I'm going to get a lot of money in the bank Monday. And after that I'm going to get a lot more, too. I'll be rolling in wealth soon. I'll give you more pay if you won't quit."

"More pay won't make any difference now. It's too late for that. I want to work for the new people."

"What new people are you talking about, Martha? Is it anybody I know? If somebody I know has sneaked behind my back and talked you into quitting and going to work for them for more pay—"

"It's some new people in town who said they'd pay me right to work for them. They bought one of those fine new brick houses over there across the road and everything's brand-new in the kitchen and all over the house with nice new carpets everywhere and no old plank floors to scrub like here. They've got television in the kitchen for me to look at and an electric dishwasher so I won't have to wash dishes myself and a vacuum cleaner and all kinds of up-to-date things like that all over the house."

"What do those people do to have so much money?"

"They own a new store on Broad Street where they said I could buy all the dresses and clothes I want for only half-price. Their two children stay at school all day and I won't have to get to work till three o'clock in the afternoon to fix up the house and cook their dinner and then I can get off work at nine o'clock. They live late like that and I won't have to go to work till the middle of the afternoon. They said it'll be just the same in summer, too, because their children go off to camp somewhere then and I'll have a full day off every week and never have to work more than six hours for the high pay I'll get. You know yourself you've had me working here from six-thirty in the morning to nearly nine o'clock at night."

"They sound like Yankees to me," Aimee said crossly. "What's their name?"

"Mr. and Mrs. Silversteen."

126

"Uh-huh! I knew it! I just knew it! It's as plain as night from day. They're Jews—and Yankee Jews at that. I've been suspicious ever since you started talking like that. Pure white Yankees are bad enough. But Yankee Jews are worst of all. Yankee Jews are richer than the rest of us and somehow they know how to get the best of everything with their money. I've looked in the Bible but I never found anything that said they ought to be better off than anybody else. You know how it is, Martha. They move here and start spoiling the colored as fast as they can by giving you people more pay and shorter hours than our white people can afford. That's the trick they use to spoil your race so you won't work for us no more. I've got a good mind to tell the right people on you."

"Miss Mamma Aimee, I told you I'm not scared of those White Cross people like I used to be. The times have changed for the colored and we don't have to live scared now."

"But working for the Yankee Jews from the North instead of for the Mangrums and other good families—"

"I don't care who it is who pays me right and makes it a better job. That's why I'm not going to keep on working here like I've been doing when I can go over there to that new place and not put up with all you make me do here—besides all the fussing at me I get. And they said there won't be any cockroaches slithering around in the pantry and coming out the cracks in the kitchen walls, neither. That's what made me as pleased as anything else they said."

"I resent that about them saying they don't have cockroaches in their pantry and kitchen. They're bragging about living in brand-new houses and trying to make people like you think they're better than the good families who live in fine old mansions like this one. That's why I resent every word about cockroaches. That's a whopping insult to me."

"It's only the truth, Miss Mamma Aimee. You know how it is in this old house. I'm scared to sit down in a chair in the

127

kitchen to rest where those cockroaches might run up my legs."

Closing her eyes and moaning resignedly, Aimee's head began moving slowly back and forth.

"I don't know why the wisdom of fate turned against me and treats me this way," she said presently, opening her eyes and looking at Martha with a pathetic drooping of her fleshy cheeks and jowl. Her voice was weak and quavering with discouragement. "I've always trusted the wisdom of fate and relied on it and now it's turned against me when I need it the most. It's a pity I went and sold that land across the road so they could build fine new houses on it for the Yankee Jews and other strange people to live in and torment me like they do. They're moving here in droves and taking the country away from all the fine old families like the Mangrums. They're hard-hearted people with no family traditions like ours and don't even care what happens to us now. They don't have pride, neither. They'd sell their houses to the colored and let them live there, too. Before they came, everybody used to be friendly neighbors, but those new people treat me like a stranger and don't even wave to me on the veranda when they drive past in their shiny new cars."

Martha picked up some of the dishes and carefully placed them on her tray without a disturbing sound.

"I'm all fagged out trying to argue with you, Martha," Aimee said sorrowfully after watching her for a while. "When are you going to desert me and go to work for them?"

"I want to quit right now tonight but I know I'll have to stay and work out the notice if you make me. I don't want it held against me that I quit you and wouldn't stay to work out the notice."

Aimee held her breath momentarily before sighing deeply.

"Martha, I feel so sorry for you that I don't want to make you keep on working here for me for another week or two

128

weeks. But if you'll stay and work for just one more day, it'd be the nicest favor you could do. It's one of our best Mangrum traditions to have all the family together at Sunday dinner and I'd feel like it was the end of the world if you didn't cook it for us just tomorrow."

"I'll do that for you, Miss Mamma Aimee. I know how you feel about that. You go on off to the church preaching in the morning. Then when you get back, I'll have the Sunday dinner all fixed. I'll fix fried chicken and mashed potatoes and gravy and all. I sure do appreciate it that you won't make me work out the notice."

Aimee, with laborious-sounding grunts and groans, slowly lifted herself from the chair and went toward the doorway. She stopped and looked back when she heard Martha humming happily to herself.

"I don't reckon you'll be going to preaching at Pastor Purdy's church, will you, Miss Mamma Aimee?" In her happy mood, Martha was smiling broadly with the gleam of her white teeth as she talked. "Pastor Purdy said he'd lose his job at the gas station if he didn't close up his church and work all day Sunday. He sure is a strange man. I never heard of a preacher closing up his church before so he could go to work at a gas station."

"Well, he said he had his reason for it and it must be a good one. But it's going to make me feel like a heathen infidel going to Sunday church while Pastor Purdy's working at that Gene Infinger's filling station and can't be doing the preaching and praying. That's bad enough, but the worst is that I'll have to sit and listen to the Methodist preacher instead of him. Anyhow, I've made up my mind about one thing."

"What's that, Miss Mamma Aimee?"

"If that Methodist preacher's wife follows me around and won't give me the chance to speak to him privately about religion this time, I'm going to turn right around and slap her

129

nasty face. I never could get the full benefit of the beauty of religion when the preacher's wife acted like she thought I was fixing to get him off somewhere out of sight and lift up my skirt for him. When a preacher's wife acts like that, it makes me so mad I feel like doing it right there and then in front of her for pure spite. I wish it was a law that preachers couldn't get married—that'd put an end to the meddling those women do."

Martha laughed. "Ain't that the truth! I wouldn't say preachers' wives don't do like that anywhere you go. I don't know why it is, but I've seen the preacher's wife do like that plenty of times at my own church."

"Well, that's the good thing about Pastor Purdy not having a wife. I could lift up my skirt for him and never have to worry about something like that."

Martha laughed again. "He sure acts like he wants somebody to lift up her skirt for him."

A glowing smile came to Aimee's round pink face.

"Martha, I have the best time talking to you of anybody I know. We like to talk about the same things, too, and that's what's so good about it. You make it so friendly we can talk about anything. It's just like me talking to another me. When you said that just now, how could you tell about what Pastor Purdy wanted done?"

"I could notice him looking at me out the corners of his eyes like he wanted me to lift up for him when he was here eating his breakfast this morning. I can tell when a man gets that notion."

"He's a white man, Martha. I'm surprised you'd say such a thing. He's not your color."

"Maybe so, but he sure acted color-blind with that on his mind. I know he wants to get to Miss Connie—I've seen him looking at her like that. But if she won't let him, he's going to have such a big thing real soon that he'll poke wherever he can."

130

Aimee drew in her breath and held it as long as she could. Then she began shaking her finger at Martha.

"Don't you dare, Martha Washington! You leave him alone! He's for me to take care of!"

Leaving abruptly, Aimee went to the parlor to sit down. When she got there, she was too upset to stay there with nobody to talk to and she went to the veranda. Before she could sit down in one of the chairs, she heard Graham talking in a loud voice to somebody in the front yard. She called to Graham to find out why he sounded so angry, but he did not answer her, and she sat down to wait for somebody to come to talk to her. Sitting there, feeling more upset and lonely as time went by, she began to be concerned about Raley, wondering where he was and what he was doing and hoping he would soon come to sit beside her.

It was a moonlight evening. There was a comfortable warm moistness in the spring air, with only a faint odor of miasma drifting across the veranda, and she sat there listening dreamily to the rhythmic sounds of the croaker frogs at the nearby pond. As she watched the glow of city lights in the distance, she began wondering where Connie was at that time of night.

Even though she had tried to keep the thought out of her mind, Aimee knew that Connie was having a date and would probably spend the night with a man somewhere in the city. However, she would not let herself believe that Connie was the prostitute Katie had accused her of being. Even so, she knew that Connie would not be staying out all night only to go to a restaurant for dinner with somebody or to a nightclub to dance.

Determined not to let herself think of Connie being paid for a date, Aimee easily convinced herself that Connie would only spend the night with a man who was in love with her and might ask her to marry him. Aimee was still hopeful that Connie would stay at home at least one more night before she went back to Savannah so Raley could make love to her again.

She still had not given up hope that Connie would marry Raley and not go back to Savannah, but, now that Connie was spending another night somewhere in Augusta, she was afraid it would be less likely to happen.

Aimee could hear Graham again talking to somebody, and this time his voice was even more loud and angry in tone. She got up and called to him a second time, asking him what he was doing and why he was so angry. When Graham still did not answer her, and knowing that Russ and Woody had left, it worried her to think he was talking like that to Raley.

Getting up and looking across the yard in the moonlight, she could see Graham and Raley standing a few feet apart at the edge of the driveway. When she called to both of them by name, neither of them answered her.

While she was watching them uneasily, she saw Graham suddenly jump at Raley and knock him down with his fists. A moment later, both of them were rolling and wrestling on the ground. Carefully feeling her way down the veranda steps, she hurried across the yard while frantically begging Graham to stop fighting Raley.

"Please stop, Graham!" she called to him. "I can see what you're doing. Get up and stop hurting Pastor Purdy. You promised me you wouldn't do that. You're bigger than he is and he can't protect himself. I'm ashamed of you, Graham. You hear me?"

Aimee could see blood on Raley's face and shirt and she reached down and tried to help him get away. She was almost knocked down when their bodies suddenly rolled against her legs. Raley tried to get up, but Graham held him on the ground.

"I'm going to be mad at you, Graham, if you don't stop hurting Pastor Purdy like that! You'd better do like I tell you! I won't like you anymore if you don't stop! You want me to like you, don't you, Graham?"

132

Graham hit Raley's face with his fist once more as hard as he could. Then he got to his feet and was about to stomp Raley when his mother pushed him away.

"I'll have to stop liking you, Graham, if you don't leave him alone. Don't you want me to keep on liking you?"

Graham nodded. "But you make him go away from here and never come back again. I don't want him here. You give him everything good to eat at the table and all he wants of it. And Connie let him get on the bed with her. I'll cut his balls off him."

"You won't do any such thing! Shame on you for saying that, Graham! You'll scare the life out of him! Now, go away and leave Pastor Purdy alone. I'm going to take him in the house now and wash all that blood off his face and find a clean shirt for him. You promise me to leave him alone and not hurt him and I'll promise that you can have all you want to eat after this."

"I want all that to eat, but he'll get on the bed again with Connie if I don't cut his balls off."

"Now, Graham," his mother said patiently, patting his arm, "I want you to quit scaring Pastor Purdy by saying you'll do a thing like that to him. Connie never said he did any harm to her. They had a friendly time together, that's all."

"If he ever gets on the bed with her again—"

"Now, Graham, go sit on the veranda for a while and then I'll come sit with you. I want to tell you how Pastor Purdy got to be a preacher by listening to Billy Graham on the radio and what wisdom of fate it was that I named you Graham before I even knew there was a famous man like Billy Graham in the world. That makes Graham a fine family name and you can be proud to have the same name he does. Now, you wouldn't want to harm Pastor Purdy, because we wouldn't know how famous your name is if he hadn't come along and told us about it. I could even rename you now because of

133

that. I could name· you Billy Graham Mangrum. Wouldn't you like that?"

"No." He reached into his pocket and took out his knife. "I don't care nothing about that. I'm going to fix him so he won't get on Connie's bed again. I'll fix Billy Graham, too, if he ever comes around here and tries to do that to her."

Hurriedly grasping Raley's hand, Aimee led him across the yard in the moonlight and took him into the house.

Chapter 13

Shortly after Sunday dinner, as a fast-moving spring storm came up the river valley from the coast at midday, there was an ominous darkening of the sky and within a very short time there was a low overcast from horizon to horizon.

When the day was darkest, a screeching wind, blowing with the force of a tornado, uprooted two of the tall old oak trees in the front yard and broke many of the mimosa limbs. After the wind storm passed over, the fallen trees and limbs were left in massive windrows on the yard and driveway. There was then a short interval of calm, soon followed by violent thunder and lightning. Finally, there was a heavy downpour of rain that lasted for more than an hour and flooded the driveway and swamped most of the lowland between the house and the pond.

When the drenching rain stopped falling shortly before five o'clock, it was too chilly for anybody to want to sit on the veranda. The sky remained gloomily overcast for the rest of the day and when the darkness brought nightfall lights in the house had to be turned on as if it had been a winter evening.

Katie and Russ were upstairs watching a television program and Graham had gone to sleep in his room after eating two full helpings of everything on the table that his mother had urged him to eat. Connie was dressing to go downtown again. And Aimee, after having cried herself to sleep when Martha told her good-bye, was finally getting up from her afternoon nap.

Velma and Woody had been in the parlor all afternoon, listening to the wind and rain and talking about the prospect of a six-week engagement for the combo at a nightclub in Florida. The Florida club owner had been present at all the performances at the Midnight Go-Go the previous night and he had made Woody an offer at closing time. An appointment had been arranged for Woody to meet him at one of the motels at seven o'clock Sunday night to discuss terms and sign a contract.

While waiting for the time to leave for the motel, Woody had kicked off his shiny tan shoes and propped his bare feet on a parlor chair. Wearing only a short housecoat, Velma was stretched out lazily on the couch and singing one of the new folksongs Woody had composed. She was barelegged in the revealing thin garment and her hanging dark-brown hair fell loosely on her shoulders. Each time the buttonless housecoat fell open, she smiled demurely at Woody and wiggled her toes playfully before snuggling into it again.

There was a single short beep of a taxi horn in the driveway. Winking at Velma, Woody pointed at Connie's room overhead with his bare toes and then jerked his thumb in the direction of the taxi.

136

"I get so many ideas for songs in Miss Mamma Aimee's house that I can't do them all."

"What's it about this time? Connie again?"

He nodded. "When the taxi horn beeps for Connie's night life to begin."

"Don't you want to do one about me now instead of her? You don't want me to be jealous, do you, Woody?"

"Okay, baby, I'll forget it this time," he said, reaching for his shoes. "I don't have to use a sister-in-law to inspire me when I've got you to do it for me better. But it's time now for me to get to that motel to see the big-big man. I'm not going to be late for that deal. I don't want nothing to go wrong-wrong now. I'm going to give my ambition its first big chance to make us rich and famous. I can already see a picture of it in pretty colors and a fancy frame all around it."

"When do you think we'll be leaving for Florida, Woody? Real soon?"

"I'll see that picture when I read the contract in black and white and talk to the big man. The sooner the better, baby. I'm all ready to get hap-happy. We ought to be leaving in a day or two if we're going to open down there next Saturday night. It'll take a day or more to drive down to Florida in that rattly old car of ours. Then we'll want plenty of time to practice for the opening and get the smell of the place up the nose."

"It would be nice if I could have a new dress for the opening. I always feel like I'm singing better when I'm wearing something new."

"I've got to talk to the big-big man about some travel money to get us down there and I'll touch him for enough so you can buy yourself something. You need a knockout dress to help put us over big-big. And I mean real way-out from here big and bigger. It's the first time we've had a chance to move up and I'm going to play it for all it's worth. From now on, believe me, to hell with these three-night weekend squeeze-a-dollar jobs. I want big-big money in my pants now."

Without turning her head to look into the parlor, Connie walked past the door with only a wave of her hand. Buster could be heard starting the taxi as soon as she left the house and it was not long until he beeped the horn once more as he and Connie rode away.

"You'd better hit me hard, baby, if you're going to keep me from making up that beep-beep taxi song. I've got a tune in my head that's driving me nuts."

While Woody was leaning over Velma and kissing her, she wiggled her toes and giggled with the tickling of his beard.

"I'll make you a deal, baby," he said as he put on his shoes. "I won't do that beep-beep song about your taxi-riding sister if you'll keep warm for me till I get back. I don't like cold-cold titties. They take the healthy color out of my beard."

"I'll keep warm for you, Woody, and I'll let you do that beep-beep song, too, when you come back."

He went as far as the door and stopped.

"Wait a minute," he said, coming back to the middle of the room. "I just thought of something, baby. While I'm gone, you give Miss Mamma Aimee the big picture about Florida. She'll put on her crying act when she hears you're going to leave home and I don't want to be around when she pumps the tears. Now's a good time to tell her and get it over with. You do that for me, baby. Okay?"

"Okay. But you be sure to go to the right room at the right motel," she called to him as he was leaving the room. "I don't want to hear anything about you and Connie accidentally being at the same place. That's one song you'd better not think about doing."

"Don't worry about that picture, baby. You know you and me. You've got me occupied."

138

Velma lay on the couch looking at the ceiling while she waited to hear the sound of the car in the driveway. When she heard Woody leave in a noisy roar, she turned partly on her side and began humming the tune of one of his new songs they planned to use at the Florida nightclub. She closed her eyes until she had finished humming the tune. In a few moments she heard the sound of footsteps as her mother came into the parlor.

Aimee was still drowsy when she sat down in her favorite chair and wriggled her fleshy body until she found the position that made her comfortable. After a prolonged and satisfying yawn, she looked around the room, fully awake at last.

"I'm so glad to see you here, honey," she said, smiling happily at Velma on the couch. "Now I know I'm really right here where I belong. Something awful happened. I had a horrible dream while I was taking my nap. I can't begin to tell you how horrible it was. It was one of my worst nightmares—day or night. I dreamed I was in a far-off part of the country somewhere and didn't know how to find my way home again. Everybody I saw was a total stranger and didn't know who I was and didn't even care about finding out. They treated me like a nobody. When I told them I was a lost Mangrum, all they did was laugh at me. That was the worst part of the dream. And another bad part was that when I told them I always felt sorry for other people and needed to be felt sorry for myself, all they did was laugh at me some more.

"Well, the rest of what happened was that I was so homesick for my own house and kinfolks that I was fixing to kill myself if I couldn't find my way back home. To show how desperate I was, I shut my eyes and started walking. And then do you know what happened? The wisdom of fate guided me so I ended up right here at home. And James was here waiting for me. He said he wanted me to go live with him so he could take care of me the rest of my life. That was the good part of the dream.

"It's a terrible thing to be lost like that where there's nothing but hard-hearted strangers and not know which way to turn to find your way back to your kinfolks. I don't like having horrible dreams like that, but if I've got to, I hope and pray for the wisdom of fate to take care of me every time. What I think it was telling me in that dream was that James ought to come back home to live and that you and Connie ought never go away and leave me. That's why I wanted to kill myself in that dream and rather be dead than have to be where there's nothing but hard-hearted strangers."

"Mamma, stop talking like that," Velma told her reprovingly. "You promised me you'd stop believing everything you dream. It's not good for you to let yourself get upset like that."

"Well, honey, I can be calm about it now—now that I'm here with you in my own house. And it does make me appreciate it a lot more having you living right here all the time and not going away like James and Connie."

Velma got up, holding the housecoat tightly around her, and went to the chair beside her mother.

"Mamma, there's something I've got to tell you before you say anything more like that. It's very important."

"Don't tell me you're going to have a baby! I won't stand for it! I don't want you bringing a baby into the world who'd grow up to look and act like Woody Woodruff! I'll speak to Dr. Price about it."

"No, it's not that, Mamma."

"Then don't scold me anymore about my dreams, honey. I don't want to be without them. It's the way the wisdom of fate guides my life for me. I'd be a lost soul without them."

"That's not what I'm talking about, Mamma. It's something else. Woody and I—we're leaving in a few days."

"What?"

"We're leaving."

"I won't listen to it!"

"But it's true. Woody has a wonderful offer from a night-club in Florida and he's going to take his combo—"

"Let him go—you stay here!"

"I'm going too, Mamma. It's just what we've been hoping for and it's his first real big chance and we're not going to let it go by. He'll be playing his own songs and composing new ones all the time. I'll be arranging the music for him and singing some of the songs. Mamma, it's the most wonderful thing that could happen to us. Aren't you glad?"

Aimee's face clouded scornfully. "Florida! I've heard all about it down there. Florida! Those people down there are the dregs of humanity. It's overrun with people not like us— Yankees and Cubans and Jews and all the other foreigners you can think of. It's no place for a Mangrum. Our family has always lived right here where we belong. If they won't draft Woody Woodruff in the army and send him off to Asia or some place like that, Florida is the best place for people like Woody Woodruff to go to and never come back. Florida! Huh! That's what I think of it!"

"Mamma, I'm married to Woody and I love him and I want to go where he goes. I wouldn't stay here and let him go away and leave me for anything. We love each other, Mamma."

"It would've been just as easy for you to marry somebody from a prominent family. Who ever heard of the Wood-ruffs!"

"Maybe you don't really know what love is anymore, Mamma. Maybe you've forgotten."

Waving her hands in front of her face as if she would not listen to another word, Aimee's tears came to her eyes.

"All my life," she sobbed, "my whole life long, I've counted on my children staying with me to the end. James took it into his head to go away and leave me and won't come back to stay, and then Connie got notions in her head and left home. And now you're saying you want to leave me. I'm going to die soon. I can feel it coming on. I won't live and breathe much longer on this earth. My health is failing fast. I had an awful pain inside me last night and I can feel another pain coming on now. I'll die all alone by myself without my dear daughters to hold my hands and comfort me while I pass away. It breaks my heart to have to sit here and think about it. I'm nothing but a deserted poor old lonely forgotten woman who nobody cares about on the way to my grave."

Velma put her arms around her mother and tried to comfort her.

"Please don't talk like that, Mamma. I'll always be coming back to see you. I'll come every chance I get. Just send for me and I'll come running. I promise that."

Aimee reached for Velma's hand and held it tightly.

"I felt this coming on. I had a hunch about it. Something told me you'd be leaving me soon. That's why I wanted Pastor Purdy to move in and stay—I just can't stand being lonely. I'd do anything to keep him from moving out now."

"Anything except marry him—I hope," Velma told her mother with a firm shaking of her head. "You'd be better off being lonely than marrying somebody with his hillbilly brains. Besides, Graham is here to keep you from being all alone."

"I admire Pastor Purdy for his handsome looks—if for nothing else—and that makes me feel sorry for him and want him to stay. And I'm afraid something might happen and they'll take Graham away. They could send Graham off somewhere and keep him locked up. That's what I dread to think about. I try to think about other things and keep it out of mind but it won't go away. Graham's not like other people. He's different. One of his uncles was the same way but we don't talk about that. Dr. Price told me he's different and I know it's true. He said Graham's liable to lose his temper and

142

do something dreadful any minute. Something like that happened ten years ago, but it was only a little colored girl he harmed and that's why they didn't take him away then. And we don't talk about that, either. Anyhow, Dr. Price says he ought to be sent off somewhere before another dreadful thing happens, but I can't bear to think of that."

She shoved Velma away from her with a sudden fling of her arm and then wiped the tears from her face.

"You made me forget what I'm mad about! It's Woody Woodruff! He's making all this trouble for me on purpose. I'll never forgive him. He talked you into this because he wants to take you away from me. He has no family of his own and he's doing this to break up our family so we won't be any better than he is. I never did like Woody Woodruff and I only put up with him this long because it kept you at home with me. He's almost driven me out of my mind already —playing that aggravating guitar of his all over the house and making up those trifling songs he sings about me and everything. He doesn't have respect for me or nothing. And now he can go and be gone and I hope I never lay eyes on him again as long as I live. I hate Woody Woodruff and I hope that's the last words I say on my deathbed. I hate him so much I can't even feel sorry for him like I do for other people."

Velma covered her face with both hands. "I wish you wouldn't talk like that, Mamma. It's so cruel."

"Why haven't they drafted him in the army and sent him off to some place in Asia on the other side of the world? That's where everybody like him belongs and should never come back from."

"Please stop being so cruel, Mamma," Velma pleaded. "I can't stand it."

Aimee became calm after that. There was a long interval of silence in the room while she gazed meditatively at Velma's

143

bare legs and revealing housecoat. Presently she leaned forward, moving her head remorsefully, and patted Velma's arm with a loving touch.

"Maybe I was too hasty talking like I was, honey," she said with a brightening of her round pink face. "Sometimes I get so upset and forget myself and say things I don't really mean. Don't hold that against me now, honey. For all I know, you might decide to change your mind about leaving home. Or maybe he—him—won't want you to go down there after all. Something like that could come up and happen. People do change their minds a lot. It's a natural thing to do."

"I don't want to hear any more about that, Mamma," Velma said as she got up from the chair and went back to the couch. "I've heard enough."

"Never mind now, honey. I don't want you to get upset. There're a lot of other things I can talk about while you're thinking about what I said. I'm still sorrowful about Martha leaving me after I've been so good to her and going to work for those new people over there across the road. And I feel guilty about Connie going to Savannah and learning to live like she does. Besides all that, I feel sorry for Pastor Purdy— I want to do so much for him."

"You're already doing enough for him—free room and board. Stop thinking about marrying him."

"Well, a younger woman your age would be better for him. I'd do anything, though, just to get him to stay here in the house to keep me company. If you hadn't already married Woody Woodruff—don't you think he's a real handsome man, honey?"

Drawing the housecoat around her without even answering her mother's question, Velma stretched out on the couch to wait for Woody to come back and tell her when they would be leaving for Florida. As she lay there looking at the ceiling, she began wiggling her toes and humming the tune of one of

144

Woody's songs. She could hear her mother saying something, as if talking to herself, but Aimee's voice sounded so far away that she did not even try to listen to what was being said.

After a while Velma closed her eyes and lay still. It seemed to her that she had been asleep for only a few minutes when she was awakened by the sound of somebody walking across the room. As she looked to see if Woody had come back, she saw Raley Purdy standing over her.

"I sure thought she was Connie—they look just alike to me now," Raley said, speaking to Aimee without looking at her. He was still standing beside the couch and looking down at Velma. "When you pointed at her and made that sign for me to be quiet—"

"It's all right now, Pastor Purdy," Aimee told him encouragingly. "Don't you worry about what you thought then. That won't make no difference at all now. You just sit right down there in that chair beside Velma so you and her can start getting acquainted."

"Where is Connie, Mrs. Mangrum?"

"Connie's gone off somewhere and you stay right where Velma is. Don't mind me at all. You and Velma haven't had the merest chance to get acquainted since you've been here and now's the best time for that. Don't you think Velma's beautiful? Don't you like to see her the way she is? I'm proud of the way she looks with her long brown hair and pretty housecoat and any man ought to appreciate her. She's never been plain-looking and careless with herself like some girls let themselves get. Ever since she grew up she's always looked like she's ready and willing to please any man who has the urge to appreciate her."

Raley was nodding in agreement and not taking his eyes from Velma in her revealing housecoat. Watching the eager expression on his face, she wondered what he would do if her mother were not in the room. Presently, when she saw

145

him looking at her bare legs, she wiggled her toes playfully.

"Are you going to sit up tonight and wait for Connie to come back?" she asked with a teasing smile. "If you do, you'll have a long wait, won't you?"

Raley turned quickly and looked at Aimee. "When is Connie coming back, Mrs. Mangrum?"

"Never mind about that. You just go ahead and get personally acquainted with Velma like it is now. I'm going up to my room right away and I won't be here to be a bother. I want you to feel all at ease while you're getting acquainted. And there won't be a better time than right here tonight like it is now."

When he looked down at Velma on the couch again, she slowly drew the housecoat over her with a slight shaking of her head as if gently scolding him for having seen her uncovered.

While Aimee was pushing herself from the chair, Velma left the couch and went toward the door. Raley, watching the tantalizing movement of Velma's body with the housecoat drawn tightly around her hips, followed her to the middle of the room.

"Please don't leave now, honey," Aimee begged. "I want you to stay here and entertain him. It's almost like I promised him you would. Don't go away and disappoint him."

"I'm going upstairs to my room, Mamma," Velma stated firmly. "I'm going up there to wait for Woody to come back."

"But what about me?" Raley said with an appealing look at Aimee. "Like it was—I thought—"

Chapter 14

After Velma left the parlor and was on her way to her room, Aimee went to Raley with a comforting smile and gently patted his arm.

"Maybe it's all for the best that she did go upstairs," Aimee told him, lowering her voice in an intimate tone. "There'll be a lot more privacy up there than down here in the parlor. Now, what I want to tell you is that you'll be doing me the finest favor you can think of if you'll go up there and somehow get Velma to change her mind and want to stay here instead of going off with Woody Woodruff. I'm glad to get rid of him. But not her. She said she's going off to Florida with him and I want her to change her mind so she'll stay here. I'd give anything for her to get to like you so much she won't want to go off with him. I'd been trying my hardest to think of some way to make her want to change her mind about leaving, and then you walked in. That's when I said to myself, uh-huh, it's the wisdom of fate for Pastor Purdy to walk in at the right time. Now I know you want to do the favor for me."

Raley rubbed his hands together while nervously moving the weight of his body from one foot to the other.

"What could I go about doing to get her to change her mind, Mrs. Mangrum? I don't know nothing what to do."

"Now, Pastor Purdy," she said with a sly glance and giving him a push with her elbow. "A manly man like you knows the best way to go about doing that."

"How do you mean, exactly? Pray for her?"

"No! This is no time for that. Do manly things. To start with, you can talk to her in a natural roundabout way to get her mind on something like a man can do. Women like to be talked to like that by a man. It gives women all sorts of romantic ideas and notions. Tell her how much you admire her—how pretty she is. Talk about going off on a moonlight picnic or something. That's a good way to start. And you remember about Connie the other night—when you went in her room—well, just remember she's Connie's sister and that they're alike in most ways. They even look alike except they have different color hair. That's why it won't be like Velma is a total stranger to you. You saw how pretty and cuddly she is when she was over there on the couch, and then just now when she walked out of the parlor the way she did. You just keep things like that in mind."

"That's right," he was quick to agree. "She's real pretty and everything. I'll talk to her, Mrs. Mangrum. And I'll do my best to get her to do like you want about staying here and not going off."

"You get her to do what you want her to do first. Forget

148

about me—think about what you want. That's what I'm counting on to change her mind. I'll tell you one little secret about
her. She's always been ticklish and acts real foolish when
she's giggling. You remember that now and it'll help. You're
a handsome manly man and nothing like Woody Woodruff.
She's bound to appreciate a man like you after living with
him all this time."

Aimee took his arm and led him to the hall. When they got
to the stairway, she leaned closer to him and whispered encouragingly.

"Just go on up there and knock on her door. Don't be
scared. I'm going to my room and stay there and you'll be all
by yourself with her."

First glancing cautiously around the hall to see if they were
alone, he then looked up the stairway with a nervous twitch-
ing of his lips.

"Don't forget all the things I said in the parlor," she reminded him with a gentle nudging.

"She was acting a lot like her sister—like Connie."

"And you could like Velma just as much as her."

"But Velma's a married woman, Mrs. Mangrum."

"Married to Woody Woodruff don't count."

"Where's Woody Woodruff now?"

"He went off somewhere."

"Are you sure?"

She nodded.

After Aimee had gone upstairs and closed her door, Raley
tiptoed to his room and sat down on the bed. Sitting there
holding his head in his hands, he began thinking about what
he would do after he knocked on Velma's door. By then—and
not only because he felt obligated to do Aimee a favor by
getting Velma to change her mind about leaving—he was
anxious to see Velma again just as she had been on the couch,

with her housecoat partly open and looking up at him while she wiggled her toes.

Not waiting any longer after that, he got the big box of candy from the hiding place under the bed, where he also kept his pistol and Bible, and tiptoed down the hall to Velma's room.

First he listened for some sound in the room, but he could hear nothing. After that, he knocked lightly on the door. When there was no answer, the next time he knocked a little harder.

"Who is that?" he heard Velma ask.

Instead of telling her who he was, he knocked again.

"Is that you, Woody?" she said.

He still did not speak, hoping she would open the door before he had to tell her who he was. He knocked again.

"Who is it then?" she said crossly. "Why don't you tell me who it is?"

"It's me—Raley."

"What do you want?"

"I want to come in."

"What for?"

"I've got a present to give you."

There was silence for several moments. He tried to turn the doorknob and open the door but it was locked.

"Velma, I'll give you a present if you'll open the door."

"You don't want to give me anything, Raley."

"Yes, I do. It's a present from me to you."

"Why do you want to do that?"

"Just because. If you'll open the door, I'll hand it to you."

There was a long pause, and then Velma opened the door a few inches. He could see that she was still wearing her thin housecoat and he tried to push the door farther open, but she was strong and determined enough to keep him from opening it any wider. He held up the box of candy so she could see it.

"Look, Raley. You've got it all wrong. I can't take a present from you. I'm married to Woody. Give it to Connie."

"But I want you to have it. It's candy."

She laughed. "That doesn't matter. You're all mixed up—that's for Connie. Wait until she comes home. She can take presents from you."

"It's not for her now. It's for you."

Velma opened the door a little wider but still not letting him come into the room.

"Raley, I want to tell you something. I know what you're up to and I'm sorry about the way I teased you down in the parlor. It didn't mean a thing and I shouldn't have done it. But I just couldn't help it after you came in and looked at me like you thought I was Connie. I know I teased you too much, so you thought it meant something, but I was only fooling. And I won't do it again. I promise. Now, wait for Connie to come home and give her the candy."

"Velma, you're pretty—you're so real pretty—you looked so pretty down in the parlor. I want to see you about that. Mrs. Mangrum said she wanted me to."

Meanwhile, Woody had come into the house, and when he got to the top of the stairway he saw Raley at the bedroom door. Making no sound and coming closer, he listened to what was being said. When he tapped Raley lightly on the shoulder, Raley turned around with a startled twist of his body. Then with a hard shove of his elbow, Woody walked past Raley and went to the door.

"I've got a great big picture in bloody-red color for you to look at, mister," he told Raley. "You son of a bitch! She's Connie's sister—and that's all. I heard what it's all about—and you're not getting any. Nobody's fooling around with my wife —and that includes preachers. Now, get the hell away from here and leave her alone. You ought to be thanking me down on your knees that I'm not fist-happy like Graham and beat-

151

ing hell out of you right now. But if you come fooling around her again, I'll show you how fist-happy I can get. Now, take your pretty box of candy and shove off. See the big bloody-red picture now, mister? Or do you want me to make it a better close-up for you to look at with bloody-red eyeballs?"

Graham, who had been in the dark corner of the hall ever since Raley had knocked on Velma's door, watched Raley go back to his room and put the box of candy under the bed again.

Trembling all over as he sat on the bed, Raley thought about what might have happened if he had been in Velma's room and Woody or Graham had found him with her. After that, he began to worry about what Aimee would think of him for failing to persuade Velma to stay at home.

Raley was still sitting there fumbling with his shirt buttons when he heard a loud knocking at the front door. The doorbell rang noisily after that and then again there was urgent knocking.

With the loud sounds echoing throughout the big house, everybody was soon awake, and, as if being warned by a neighbor that the house was on fire, they all hurried from their rooms to the downstairs hall.

When the veranda light was switched on, the door was opened and they saw Connie's limp body being held by a husky young man in a dark-green uniform. He was about twenty-eight years old and was tall and muscular, with light-color short hair and a broad stern face. Connie was barefooted and wrapped in a large yellow blanket.

Connie moved her head when the bright light shone in her eyes, and she stared dazedly around her.

"What's the matter with her?" Russ asked the young man in the green uniform. "Is she hurt? Has she been in a car accident? What happened?"

152

"No car accident," he said calmly. "Nothing like that. She's drunk. I want to talk to her mother—Mrs. Mangrum. Somebody take her now and put her to bed. She's in bad shape and needs help. But she'll be all right later."

Velma and Katie took Connie and helped her through the hall and up the stairway. She was wearing none of her clothing under the yellow blanket and her bright blonde hair was uncombed and tousled, but she was still clutching her large handbag.

"What in the world?" Aimee said excitedly. "What happened to her? Where's she been? And who are you?"

"Mrs. Mangrum, my name is Ed Hascum and I have my ID if you'd like to see it."

"What business is this of yours? Did you get her drunk? What kind of uniform is that you've got on? What are you, anyhow—a policeman or sheriff?"

"Mrs. Mangrum," the serious-faced Ed Hascum said patiently, "I'm the night security guard at the Red Carpet Motel up on the expressway. If you'd rather talk about this in private, we'd better go somewhere else."

"Who's your family?" Aimee demanded curtly.

"My name is Hascum. That's all."

"I never heard that name before. You must be some of the new people in town. You talk like they do."

He nodded. "I suppose so."

"Well, I want to know more about you before I'll talk to a complete stranger. Where did you come to Augusta from?"

"My wife and I came here to live about a year ago after I did a six-year hitch in the army. I was stationed at Fort Gordon part of that time and I got to know Augusta pretty well. My wife liked the climate and I got the security job at the motel because I'd had MP training. That's about all there is to say."

Aimee took him to the far end of the lighted veranda. Everybody else waited near the doorway.

"It's something disgraceful—I just know it is," Aimee said as she put both hands against her face. "But I've got to know. What is it? What did Connie do?"

"Mrs. Mangrum, your daughter was creating a disturbance at the Red Carpet Motel tonight. This wasn't the first time this week she's been there as an unregistered guest, but she hadn't made any serious trouble for us before. We've been watching her for several nights, and then tonight she ran all over the place knocking on doors and disturbing guests. Some of them were families with children in their rooms."

"Is that all?" she asked hopefully.

"No, that's not all. She was drunk and had taken off her clothes. She was completely nude in public."

"Oh, my God! Is that why she only had a blanket around her when you brought her home?"

He nodded. "Mrs. Mangrum, the motel manager knew who she was—he knew all the time that she's your daughter—and he didn't want to have her arrested not only because of your family, but also because it's not the kind of publicity that's good for the Red Carpet Motel. That kind of bad publicity keeps families with children away. And a businessman's wife wouldn't want him to stay there, either. Anyway, if the police had been called, they'd have jailed your daughter and it would've been in the newspapers because she is a Mangrum. I don't like to say it but you ought to know that she would've been charged with more than just disturbing the peace. There would've been a prostitution charge, too, after the police made their investigation. As I understand it, she has a police record downtown—something that happened about two years ago—a suspended sentence on a prostitution charge—and this time she wouldn't get off so lightly. That's why the manager told me to bring her here and turn her over to you."

154

"That's a terrible thing to say about my daughter—accusing her of what you said! I don't believe a word of it!"

"I can't make you believe it, Mrs. Mangrum, but if you want to go up to the Red Carpet and talk to the manager—"

"No, not that," Aimee said immediately. "But I want you to know that she's not what you said about her. Connie couldn't be. I won't believe it. She's a Mangrum and a respectable girl. Nobody in the Mangrum family ever had that awful thing said about them before and I resent every word you say like that about her. She told me she has dates with a lot of prominent men in Savannah, where she's a hostess in a private club, and everybody respects her because she's a Mangrum. Connie's been going downtown here since she came home for a visit and nothing like this happened before. It's an insult for anybody to say such things about Connie Mangrum."

"I'm sorry to upset you about it, Mrs. Mangrum. I just wanted you to understand why I had to bring her here in the condition she was in. And now there's one more thing. The motel manager said he wants to advise you to send her back to Savannah right away and not let her come to Augusta again. He said if she comes to the Red Carpet once more, he would have to have her arrested on sight the next time. I think that's good advice. I'd hate to have to go to court and testify that she was soliciting for prostitution at the motel."

Aimee went to the veranda railing and looked at the glow of city lights beyond Mangrum Road.

"How do you know she was doing what you said—she could've been doing something respectable—you could be making all that up!"

"There'd be no purpose in doing that, Mrs. Mangrum. And if you really want to know everything—"

"What else is there?"

"Mrs. Mangrum, a taxi driver named Buster has been bringing your daughter to the motel for dates, and she was in and

155

out of guest rooms several times every night she's been there. We know all about Buster's activity, because transporting call girls is his specialty. Anyway, there wasn't much we wanted to do about it, because we don't like to make trouble for registered guests as long as everything is kept quiet and orderly. That's the policy of the Red Carpet and most other high-class motels these days.

"But tonight it was different. Several men who are in town for a convention had your daughter at a party in one of the suites and she got drunk. That was the beginning. I had a watch on her through a parted curtain and the manager was not going to do anything about it if she stayed in the suite. But she didn't. She left there—without her clothes on—and then went from door to door asking men to invite her in for a private party. And that's when the manager decided she'd have to go. But I want you to know that I was doing what I'm employed to do when I reported to the manager what I saw through windows and when I followed her around the motel. I had nothing against her personally. It's my job.

"That's everything, Mrs. Mangrum, and now you know why I brought her home the way she was. We couldn't find her clothes. I wrapped the blanket around her because some of the men had taken her clothes for souvenirs."

Aimee turned her back to the glow of city lights.

"I don't know what to say now." She spoke as if appealing to Ed Hascum for sympathy. "I tried to think nothing like that was going on. I tried to keep it out of mind. But all the time I was afraid it was. I didn't want to believe my own daughter would be doing that. Like a common streetwalker. I'd heard gossip that she'd been in trouble with the police about that not long after she finished high school. But I wouldn't let myself believe a word of it. Now I know whose fault it is that it happened. It's mine. I wish she'd never left home and gone to Savannah—or had left home a lot sooner when she first wanted to and gone a thousand miles away. She begged to go away to college, like her brother James did, when she finished high school. But I wouldn't give her the money and let her. That's why I'm to blame. Now this has happened and it looks like we can't keep on being the fine family we used to be. I don't know what to think of myself."

Wiping some of the tears from her face, she walked away from the end of the veranda.

"I'm very sorry about all this, Mrs. Mangrum," Ed Hascum said as he went with her as far as the veranda steps. "I hope I helped some by bringing her home tonight. And I hope it never happens again—here or in Savannah or anywhere else. A pretty girl like her—"

Aimee reached for his arm, clutching it gratefully, and leaned her head on his shoulder.

"I want to take back the mean way I talked to you a while ago—you're such a fine man. And I want to thank you with all my heart for bringing her home and not letting her get arrested and put in jail. I could never get over that as long as I lived. God bless you!"

More tears were coming to her eyes. Wiping them away so she could see where she was going, she went back into the house and slowly climbed the long stairway to her room.

Chapter 15

Katie got up early Monday morning before anybody else in the house was awake and dressed herself in her best clothes with particular care and even put on her hat. She was careful not to make any disturbing sounds while dressing, and Russ was still asleep on his side of the curtain rod when she left the room.

When Katie passed Aimee's bedroom door on her way downstairs, she turned her head and would not even let herself look at it. It was the first time during the eight years she had been married to Russ that she would have to prepare her own breakfast and it was provoking that Aimee had not immediately hired another servant to take Martha's place.

After entering the kitchen, she began opening and noisily

slamming cupboard doors and drawers while looking for something to cook for her breakfast. In the end, all she could find were some shriveled potatoes and part of a loaf of bread and the coffee. She looked everywhere she could think of without finding eggs or sausage and she blamed Aimee for hiding them from her.

And then, to make her even more provoked and angry, she cut a deep gash in her thumb while slicing a potato to put into the frying pan. Tearful and angry, holding up her bleeding thumb with a napkin wrapped around it, she then burned the fingers of her other hand when she picked up the sizzling frying pan to turn over the potatoes.

After having been in the kitchen for nearly half an hour, Katie was sitting at the table and chewing some of the potatoes with a distasteful grimace when Russ came into the dining room. The thick slices of potatoes were raw on one side and scorched and charred on the other side.

Russ sat down without a word, sleepily rubbing his eyes, and waited for Katie to bring his breakfast, while she made a pretense of ignoring him as if he were not even in the same room with her. Katie looked vaguely at one of the walls and then at a crack in the ceiling and then down at her plate, but never directly at Russ.

"Where's my breakfast?" at last he demanded impatiently, speaking to her for the first time that morning. "I'm hungry. You hear?"

Unhurried and pretending she had heard nothing, she cut another bite of partly-raw potato with her knife and fork and daintily put it into her mouth.

"You know Martha left," he told her accusingly. "She's not here to cook it for me. Go on and hurry up and do something about it. And fix my potatoes right. I don't want none like you're eating. You hear?"

Katie, wrapping the blood-soaked napkin more tightly

159

around her thumb, continued chewing the thick slice of potato as if she still had not heard a word spoken.

"What's wrong with your thumb, Katie?" he asked, noticing it for the first time. "What did you do to it?"

When there was no answer, he leaned closer, squinting his eyes and staring at her face. She still ignored him.

"What the hell's the matter with you, Katie?" he demanded in a loud voice. "God damn it! Stop that acting like you're deaf and dumb. I want my breakfast. Now hurry up about it. You hear?"

When she did not get up and go to the kitchen after that, and still would not speak to him, Russ leaned back in his chair and regarded her with a bewildered grin. That was when he noticed that instead of one of her ordinary house dresses, she was wearing her best clothes, which she always wore to Sunday church services and funerals, and the new hat she had decorated with a blue ribbon and yellow spring daisies. She had never before gone downtown to shop that early in the morning, and he sat there trying to think why she would be wearing her best clothes and a new hat at such a time.

"What are you dressed up like that for?" he asked curiously, his manner suddenly no longer fretful and complaining. "Where are you going at this time of day? Why won't you say something, Katie? It's not like you not to talk now like you've been doing for eight years. Say something. What are you mad about?"

She carefully scraped some of the black char from a potato slice before putting it into her mouth.

"Then tell me who you're mad at. Is it me?"

Katie dropped her fork on the plate with a loud clatter as she glared at him.

"Don't speak to me again, Russell Mangrum. Stop annoying me. I'm not going to answer your prying questions about my personal affairs."

160

"Why won't you, Katie?"

"You'll find out soon enough."

"I will? What will I find out?"

She would say nothing more after that.

"God damn it, Katie!" he shouted angrily.

Aimee, wearing one of her bright-green, floral-print house dresses, came into the dining room and seated herself at her place at the head of the table. After making herself comfortable in the chair, she looked first at the empty plate in front of Russ and then at the partly-raw and charred potatoes on Katie's plate.

"Russell, go fry me and you some sausage," she told him. "You'll find the sausage hidden under that big tin pan on the pantry shelf behind all those empty boxes. It's where nobody could find it and put rat poison in it to kill me off. There're some people I'm smart enough not to trust when my back is turned."

Russ stood up to go to the kitchen. "Do you want me to fry some for Katie, too?" he asked.

"No. She's already fixed her own breakfast."

Katie drew her thin lips tightly across her face.

He glanced at Katie. "If she wants some, I don't mind fixing it for her."

"No, and that's that!"

Russ started toward the kitchen.

"And when you finish making the sausage cakes for me and you," Aimee told him precisely, "leave the rest of it on the kitchen table till I go there and find a new hiding place for it."

After Russ had gone to the kitchen, Aimee reached for the coffeepot. Katie was quick to move it beyond her reach.

"What did you do that for, Katie?"

Katie smiled to herself.

"Pass me that coffee, Katie!"

"This is my coffee. I made it for myself."

"It's my coffeepot!"

"But you didn't make the coffee in it and I did."

Aimee slowly raised her body upright in the chair. She opened her mouth, breathing rapidly, and it was several moments before she could speak.

"What kind of talk is that?" she then demanded.

"I'm nobody's servant—that's what."

"After all I've done for you—"

"That makes no difference."

Aimee drew a deep breath and puffed her cheeks until she could hold her breath no longer.

"Well, of all things! I can hardly believe my own ears! I never thought I'd hear such mean talk to me in my own house!"

"You heard it now. I'd never lower myself to be a common servant for you."

"That's the limit, Katie Snoddyhouse!" Aimee said in anger. "The absolute limit! I've never been treated like this before in all my life. And after me feeling sorry for you like I have for eight years. I invite you to get out of my house right away and never come back. I don't care now how sorry I ever was for you. I don't want you here no more and I don't care where you go. Now, get up and get out!"

Katie smiled to herself with a toss of her head. She carefully mashed a slice of potato before putting it into her mouth.

"I just as much as got on my knees once before and begged you to stay here and not move out," Aimee told her, "but this time—I'll—I'll—get behind you and push you out of my house if you don't get up and go yourself. That's how unwelcome you are now, Katie Snoddyhouse! And don't sit there and pretend you don't understand plain talk!"

"You don't have to bother yourself saying that. I'm leaving as fast as I can pack up and leave."

162

Aimee looked at her in silence for a moment.

"Did you say you've already made up your mind to leave? And that's what you're really going to do? What made you decide that, Katie?"

"I don't mind telling you why—if you can stand hearing the truth. No decent-minded person would stay another day in this shameful house after that disgusting thing last night. I was so ashamed of myself for helping to take Connie Mangrum upstairs and putting her to bed last night the way she was naked that I had to wash my hands with soap and hot water three times before I felt clean. That's why I think too much of myself to stay any longer under the same roof with a common somebody like her. Being naked at a motel with strange men! Even a decent married woman wouldn't let herself be seen like that in her own house by her own husband! Everybody in Augusta is going to hear how she was brought home naked and drunk last night from that motel. Scandal like that is talked about all over the city and I couldn't hold up my head if people knew I lived in the same house with a sinful woman like her. People who saw me at church on Sunday would snicker and talk about me behind my back like I was a common somebody myself. It's disgusting. I despise all you Mangrums and Connie Mangrum is no better than—than—"

"Shut your mouth, Katie Snoddyhouse! Don't you keep on talking about Connie like that!"

"Don't you worry. I'm not going to. I've said the last word about her. I wouldn't defile my mouth talking about her with another word."

Russ came from the kitchen with a platter of fried sausage cakes. After sitting down and helping himself, he passed the platter to Aimee.

"Russell, are you going to leave, too?" Aimee asked him anxiously. "Are you, Russell?"

When he hesitated instead of answering immediately, Aimee reached over the table and gripped his arm.

"Please don't say so, Russell. I couldn't stand to hear it. I couldn't live another day without my close relatives like you here in the house with me. You're the only brother-in-law I've got. You know how much I appreciate you. I don't want to be left here alone in the world."

Russ glanced at Katie, and then he began shaking his head while hungrily chewing a large bite of sausage.

"I don't know the first thing about it, Aimee. She hasn't told me nothing—except that I'd find out something soon enough. All I know now beside that is what I heard her say while I listened in the kitchen. I asked her a while ago why she was all dressed up with a hat on to go somewhere. But I can't make her talk any more than that."

Katie poured herself another cup of coffee and then moved the pot farther away from Aimee's reach.

Instead of becoming angered again when Katie once more refused to share the coffee, Aimee smiled at her with a brief pleasantness.

"Katie, where are you going to move to? Are you going to leave town or stay somewhere in Augusta?"

"I don't know that it's any of your business what I do. But it makes me proud to tell you, anyhow. I'm moving to my brother's house to live with respectable people. I phoned my brother early this morning and he's coming for me any minute now and carry out everything of mine so none of my belongings will get contaminated another day in this house. I'm going to live with my decent relatives in a decent way from now on. And as soon as I get out of this house I'll start living down the disgrace of being associated with you Mangrums all this time."

Aimee pointed at Russ. "What about him? Are you going to make Russell go with you?"

"I am not!"

"But you're married to him. What are you going to do about that?"

"I'm leaving him once and for all and you can have him."

Russ's mouth dropped open. His eyes blinked bewilderedly as he looked back and forth at Aimee and Katie.

"But Russell said he didn't know—"

"He'll know now. I'm going to see a lawyer as soon as I can go downtown and tell him to get me a divorce as fast as the law allows and have my undefiled family name restored to me. I'd never be able to hold up my head in public again if I had to keep the Mangrum name. I'd be ashamed to walk down Broad Street and have people look at me and know I was one of the Mangrums. I'm going to be Katie Snoddyhouse and hold up my head with pride."

A beaming smile came to Aimee's round pink face.

"Well, I'm tickled all over to hear that. I wish you'd done it sooner, but it's better now than never. You started out being Katie Snoddyhouse and that's all you've ever been as far as I'm concerned. And when you die, have them put your Snoddyhouse name on your tombstone. I don't want anybody to go to the cemetery and see our name on it. You've never been a true Mangrum like the rest of us."

While Russ was sitting there with a cautious grin, as if afraid Katie might change her mind about getting a divorce, there were several sharp blasts of an automobile horn in front of the house. Katie, without even a parting glance at Russ or Aimee, quickly got up and left the dining room.

Gradually grinning more happily, Russ turned his head and listened to the sound of Katie's footsteps as she went through the hall.

Leaning over the table and reaching for his arm, Aimee patted him comfortingly.

"Russell, I don't want you to feel bad about what she said—

getting a divorce from you. You've been married to her so long you might miss her being around all the time—at first, I mean. But that won't last. I'm here and we're used to each other now—"

"Me? Feel Bad? Miss her?" he said at once, leaning back in his chair. His broad grin had become a happy smile on his face. "After sleeping in bed with her for eight years for nothing? Good God Almighty! After all this time!"

"Russell, there's no law against a brother-in-law taking out a marriage license—"

"I couldn't never feel better than I do right now," he said elatedly, too excited to have heard what Aimee said. "You wouldn't know about it unless somebody told you. She wouldn't give me a treat even once in all those eight years. And all that time me sleeping in a cold bed with an iron curtain-rod down the middle that had big brass rings around so it made a racket if I got too close to it. I don't know what it was about her, but she had me doing everything her way right from the start—even getting married to her when I didn't want to. It was like she was conjuring me all the time. The only thing she'd let me do was go bowling—and I sure made good use of that."

"So that's what happened to my curtain rod that I've been looking for all this time!"

Russ nodded. "That's what started me going to Telfair Street. I had to do something like that about it. And from now on I can go there as much as I please and won't never have to go bowling again for an excuse to leave the house at night. I'm never going nowhere near another God damn bowling alley again as long as I live. I'm sick and tired of lifting up those big heavy balls and trying to hit what looks like nothing but some belly-fat sticks of wood."

"Well, I'll declare! Using my curtain rod to do that to you! So that's why you went bowling so much! Who do you go to see on Telfair Street, Russell?"

"She's just a friend of mine."

"What's her family name?"

"Smith."

"That's a real ordinary name, Russell. If you'll change your mind—I mean if you want to stay here with me instead—well, like I said, we're used to each other now and with Katie gone—"

Aimee was interrupted by loud thumping on the stairway as Katie and her brother moved some heavy packing boxes down to the lower hall. (*I think I know how it happened that Katie and Russ got married. Katie was a frisky good-looking girl eight years ago and Russ was crazy for somebody like her. What Katie did was hold out for marriage, though, because all she had in mind was marrying into the Mangrum wealth for her own benefit. Russ was dumb about it, like he is about everything else, and he thought he was really going to get it good by marrying her. But she outsmarted him. The minute they got married, like a whore trying to get one more dollar, Katie kept on holding out to get some Mangrum money first— which she never did. As everybody knows, Aimee held on to it and wouldn't share it because she had this thing about Russ and wanted him for herself and hated Katie for marrying him. There wouldn't have been none of this trouble if Russ had gone ahead and married Aimee right after her husband Ralph died. But you can't put two women like Aimee and Katie in the same house, with Russ Mangrum in the middle, and expect anything different. The way it ended up, Russ got cheated out of everything, money and all. But it's Russ's fault—being dumb enough to let Katie fool him to start with. And then all that time he couldn't get up and leave Katie because he wanted to stay in the house to be there to get a share of the Mangrum money. It's been a hell of a mess all the way around for everybody. I tell you, these old families will stay in a tangle either till they get broken up and scattered—or die off.*) Realizing what was happening in the hall,

Aimee got up from the table and hurried from the dining room.

"Come on with me, Russell," she called urgently. "Katie might be taking away things that belong to me and I want you to help me stop her. I don't trust her one minute behind my back."

When they got to the bottom of the stairway, Aimee opened one of the boxes and the first thing she saw was a pair of sun-faded brown curtains that Katie had taken from her bedroom window.

"Get your hands off my personal things!" Katie yelled in her high-pitched voice. "I've got a right to take what belongs to me!"

"No, you don't Katie Snoddyhouse! These are my curtains and they're not leaving my house!"

Aimee jerked the curtains from the box and held them behind her back.

"I made those curtains myself with my own hands," Katie said, trying to take them from Aimee.

Aimee easily pushed her aside.

"Maybe you made them, but that's all. I bought and paid for the cloth and you used my sewing machine. That makes them mine and you quit trying to grab them away."

"You're stingy and mean about everything—just like you are about the money I never got for marrying your brother-in-law!"

Katie carried the box to the veranda and then went back upstairs to get something else. When she was out of sight, Aimee hid the curtains under the couch in the parlor.

When Aimee and Russ got to the front door, they saw that Katie's brother, Fred Snoddyhouse, had backed his heavy truck across the lawn all the way to the veranda steps. The big truck had made deep ruts in the rain-soaked lawn and the rear wheels were mired hub-deep in the soft earth of the

168

flower bed that bordered the brick walkway. While Aimee was looking at the damage to the lawn and flowers, Katie and her brother came out of the house with two more large packing cases.

"Just look at what you've gone now and done to my beautiful flowers—you—you—Snoddyhouses you!" Aimee pushed Katie backward against the side of the truck. "My beautiful flowers are ruined and it's your fault!"

Fred Snoddyhouse gripped Aimee's arm and pulled her away from his sister. He was a small man, much shorter in height than Aimee, but he was quick and agile and easily shoved her aside. Fred had a wide, reddish moustache that gave him a fierce appearance when he was provoked.

"You leave her alone, Mrs. Mangrum," he warned her, taking a threatening stand and facing her defiantly. There was an angry flush of his pale skin from his neck to his shiny bald head. "Don't you dare touch her again like that."

"You don't know who you're talking to, Fred Snoddyhouse! You don't have no right to come to my house and ruin my flowers and order me around!"

"I don't care who you think you are—a Mangrum or nothing. You keep your hands off Katie and don't do that again."

"What do you think you'd do?"

"You try it and see."

Aimee hurried to the veranda steps.

"Graham!" she called as loudly as she could. "Graham! Come help me! Hurry, Graham!"

She then went to the corner of the house and got a garden hoe. When she came back, Russ tried to take it from her to keep her from slashing Katie or Fred with the sharp blade. Aimee kept her grip on the handle until she saw Graham coming from the house.

"Graham! Look what they've done!" she called to him, pointing at the flower bed. "Make them go away!"

Graham lunged at Fred, hitting him with both fists, and knocked him backward against the truck. A trickle of blood came from Fred's nose.

"You hit me again, Graham Mangrum, and I'll beat hell out of you," Fred said as he wiped the blood from his nose and moustache with the back of his hand. "I came here to haul Katie's things away and not to pick a fight with you. Now, stay away from me and leave me alone or you'll wish you had. I'm not scared of you."

Before Fred could protect himself, Graham began hitting his face with both fists again. Fred dropped to one knee and then locked his arms around Graham's legs. They both fell to the ground and wrestled on the soggy lawn. Fred soon got both hands on Graham's throat and tried to choke him.

"Don't you hurt Graham, Fred Snoddyhouse!" Aimee cried out, taking the hoe from Russ and trying to hit Fred with it. "I'll have you arrested for this if you don't stop!"

Katie, frightened, hurriedly got into the truck and locked the cab door.

Graham got his knees against Fred's chest and heaved him with such force that Fred went sprawling on his back. Jumping at him then, Graham tried to stomp his face. Fred rolled over and quickly got to his feet.

"You'd better get away from here in a hurry, Fred," Russ warned him. "I can't stop Graham when he loses his temper like this. He's too strong for me to hold him back."

One of the boxes of Katie's belongings was still on the veranda, but she begged her brother to hurry and leave without it. Fred got into the truck and started the engine as quickly as he could. With a spinning of the rear wheels in the flower bed that splattered mud on Aimee, Fred drove the heavy truck away and made two more deep ruts in the rain-soaked lawn.

By then, everybody in the house had been awakened by

170

the loud commotion in the front yard. Velma and Woody were looking down from their second-floor window and Connie and Raley were at two of the other windows.

"What the hell you folks doing down there?" Woody yelled from his window. "It's too early in the morning for me to think up a song about whatever the hell you're doing. Go away and come back when I'm ready to do it."

Chapter 16

After Russ and Graham went back into the house, Aimee, still tense with anger and short of breath, sat down on the veranda steps and gazed dejectedly at her crushed and uprooted flowers.

She sat there alone for a long time, dabbing at the tears in her eyes and trying to wipe off the mud that had been splattered on her face.

The man in the blue coveralls who was working with the big yellow bulldozer on the other side of Mangrum Road had shut off the noisy diesel engine while he watched the fight between Graham and Fred. The monotonous grinding hum began again when he went back to work scraping and terracing the site where another new house was to be built.

Aimee was still sitting on the steps and trying to shut out the exasperating sound of the bulldozer on the land that had previously belonged to her when Cato Boykin stopped his car in the driveway.

All anger quickly vanished and her face brightened when she saw Cato, carrying a bulging tan briefcase, get out of his car and come up the walkway to the house.

"Have you got that money for me, Cato?" she called out eagerly, long before he reached the steps. "You'd better have it. You said I could have it Monday and that's what today is."

"Aimee, if it's Monday you can be sure the money is here, because I'm a man of my word." He sat down on the step beside her, smiling in his friendly manner, and patted the tan briefcase. "And you're right about it being Monday. I know it is because my wife made me go to church yesterday. It looks like a man my age ought to be able to have a say-so about going to church, but my wife won't let me have it that way. I got up early yesterday morning before she was awake and tiptoed around and put on my old clothes to go fishing down the river and then she woke up and grabbed me before I could get out of the house."

As he looked at her then, he noticed for the first time that she had smears of mud on her face.

"Looks like you've been doing some real serious gardening this morning, Aimee. It's a beautiful morning for gardening— a balmy day and a mild sun and the invigorating juices of spring bubbling in fauna and flora. It's a great day to be alive in. I wish I could've stayed at home today and puttered around among my roses. But of course I'd never let myself neglect strict attention to your affairs. I'm as conscientious about that as my wife is about my religious welfare on Sunday mornings."

Pointing at the deep holes and crushed plants in the flower bed, Aimee told him about Katie saying she was leaving Russ

173

to get a divorce and then about Fred Snoddyhouse backing his heavy truck across the lawn into the soft dirt when he came for her.

"Well," Cato said with a sympathetic movement of his head, "I'm sorry to see somebody come here and churn up your flower bed like that. It's a shameful thing for anybody to do. But at least there'll be one less mouth for you to feed if Katie does stay away. How does Russ feel about her divorcing him?"

"He'd better feel like I do—glad to get rid of her. But he won't be going after her and trying to get her to come back— he told me so. Now, give me the money, Cato. Every last penny of that hundred dollars you gave me is all spent and gone."

"Aimee, don't tell me that you gave any of it to that evangelist. Did you? Tell me the truth."

"I didn't have to. Pastor Purdy has a job at Gene Infinger's filling station. I hate to see him have anything to do with that mean Infinger man, but he said it was the only job he could get."

"What about his preaching?"

"He had to put that aside for a while. But he's going to open up his church later and start preaching again."

"Aimee, tell me the truth. You're not thinking about marrying him, are you?"

"Now why would you ask a question like that?"

"Because you've been doing foolish things for several years now and it's time for you to come to your senses and put a stop to it."

"But I feel sorry for him."

"You won't feel half as sorry for him as I will for you if you do such a foolish thing."

"Keep your advice to yourself and give me the money, Cato," she told him abruptly.

174

Cato opened the briefcase and took out a large bundle of papers. Wetting the tip of his finger, he carefully looked through the file to make sure the papers were in proper order.

"I thought maybe you'd want my advice before you'd marry any man half your age and younger than your oldest son. And I'm sure you already know what my advice would be. But, immediate matters immediately. That's been my life-long professional procedure."

He handed her one of the papers and uncapped his fountain pen for her.

"Now, Aimee, as your attorney, I advise you to take the time to read every word so you'll know exactly what you're doing before you sign anything. And if there's anything you don't clearly understand, I'll be glad to explain it to you. Some legal terminology can be confusing even to a lawyer until it's simplified and translated into the comprehensible."

"Don't get me all mixed up talking like that. Just tell me what this paper is for. That's all I want to know."

"That is the note to be signed for the bank loan of one thousand dollars and the next document encumbers your property as security until the loan is repaid. The other papers for your signature follow in sequence and I'll explain as we go along. This's not the usual way to handle such matters, but I arranged with the bank to bring all the documents here to you and have them executed simultaneously, so to speak. I personally assumed responsibility to handle it like this so you wouldn't have to make several trips downtown. Now you'll have the money promptly, just as we discussed in my office the other day."

"It's a lot for me to have to do to get a thousand dollars."

"But it's not your money, Aimee. It's the bank's money and this is the usual method for arranging a loan."

"Why isn't it my money? I'm going to spend it."

"Well, I'll try to explain that as we go along."

175

Slowly moving her head from side to side, Aimee frowned thoughtfully for several moments.

"I don't know if I want to trust you like this, Cato Boykin. You might be cheating me and fixing to put a lot of my money in your own pocket. I've heard of lawyers getting widows to sign something and tricking them out of money like that. There's that poor Mrs. Button who lives not far from here. When she was widowed about a year ago, a lawyer got her to sign something and—"

"I know all about that, Aimee, and there is some question about the ethics involved. There are many lawyers and now and then one will take advantage of a client. But I want you to trust me and rest assured that I'd never do such a thing. Ralph Mangrum had complete faith in my integrity while he was alive. And as a matter of fact, he even trusted me during the last years of his life by giving me unqualified power of attorney. However, if it'll give you peace of mind, I'll gladly be bonded for any sum you want to set."

After a few moments of indecision, she finally signed the two documents with her scrawling signature and handed them back to Cato.

"Now I want my money," she told him.

"Here it is, Aimee. These are two checks drawn to your order. One is for nine hundred dollars, which I will deposit in your account today. And one is for a hundred dollars which you can endorse over to me as repayment of the money I advanced out of pocket in my office last week."

He placed the briefcase on Aimee's lap for her to use while endorsing the checks.

"Later, of course," he remarked in a casual manner as he put the endorsed checks into his briefcase, "there will be a modest fee you can pay me for legal services. But we won't discuss that until the whole matter is concluded."

"I haven't made up my mind how much I want to pay you."

"Aimee, it's customary for the attorney to set the fee on the basis of—"

"I've got my own customs. Maybe it's not worth paying you anything for. All you ever do is hand me papers to sign. I don't call that much work."

Cato looked straight ahead, listening to the grinding hum of the bulldozer across the road.

"Well, now, Aimee," he said a few moments later, "I'm glad to help you like this and I've been a friend of the family all these years. I wouldn't think of asking you to pay me an exorbitant fee. But at the same time there's a great deal of legal work involved and certain expenses connected with it. For example, the cost of the appraisal of your property—"

"I'll tell you if I ever want to talk about it."

After wiping the perspiration from his forehead, he put on his hat to shade his face from the warm sun.

"Now, there's just one more paper for you to sign, Aimee," he said with a businesslike rustle of the documents, "and then all these matters will be taken care of for the present. This is a letter of intent, so to speak, authorizing me to negotiate the sale of your property. We've already verbally agreed about this and signing the document is merely a formality. I'm happy to tell you that three real estate developers are preparing to submit offers as soon as the appraisal is placed in their hands. This means that I expect to have some very good news for you perhaps within a week or ten days. This is much sooner than I'd made allowance for. But I'm not surprised your property has stirred up this interest and I'm confident the amount of money it's going to bring will surprise you. You're on the verge of being a very rich woman, Aimee."

She looked briefly at the paper and then thrust it away without signing it.

"I've changed my mind," she said shortly. "I'm not going to do it. I won't sell another inch of my property."

"Aimee, you can't change your mind now. It was verbally agreed between us that I was to offer the entire property for sale at the best obtainable price and I've begun negotiations in good faith. And this loan of a thousand dollars at the bank—"

"Nobody can keep me from changing my mind. And I can always change my mind about changing my mind, too."

"But in the business world—certain practices in good faith —verbal agreements—"

"You stay in that world if you want to and I'll stay in mine. I'm just not going to do it now."

"But why? You authorized me—"

"For the best reason there is." Tears began rolling down her cheeks. "Everybody's going away and leaving me. Connie's going back to Savannah and Velma's going to Florida to stay and James left a long time ago. And now Russell might be leaving to live with some woman named Smith on Telfair Street. I've got to keep my own house. It's all I've got left."

"There's Graham. You and Graham could move to a fine apartment downtown and have a maid and you wouldn't be lonely like you'd be in this big house."

"That's not what I want."

"Then what do you want?"

"I want James—I want to keep the house for him to come back to. I miss him so much. He's my firstborn. He's always been my favorite. If he'd only live somewhere near—just so I'd be close to him—to know he was there—"

"Then you can go to Atlanta and live near him."

"He's never asked me to. And I'd be afraid about Graham in a strange place with strange people all around. The least little thing could make him lose his temper—then something awful could happen—like it did once before—that little colored girl—and they'd take him away and lock him up somewhere."

178

She put her head on Cato's shoulder.

"Aimee, for the good of everybody concerned, if Graham could be sent somewhere—"

She sat up erectly, pushing Cato away from her.

"No! I know what you're saying! I won't listen to it! If only somebody would stay here—Connie or Velma or James—then I could die in peace when the time comes. I tried to get Connie to marry Pastor Purdy and stay here. Then I tried to get Velma to leave Woody Woodruff and stay here where Pastor Purdy is. I know it wasn't a moral thing to do—it was a sinful thing—but I had to. And all the scheming I did didn't amount to anything and all the praise I heaped on the Mangrum family to make everybody proud of the Mangrum name didn't do a bit of good, either. Nobody cares about the Mangrum family anymore—not even my own children. And I put up with Katie Snoddyhouse for eight long years just so Russell would stay here, and now he acts like he's going to leave too. I hinted this morning about him marrying me and staying here, but that didn't do a bit of good. Now I'm the only one left to look after Graham."

Cato began putting his papers back into his briefcase. It was late in the morning and he had been away from his office for nearly two hours. When he stood up and looked down at Aimee with her round pink face wet with tears, he tried to think of something comforting to say before he left. He put his hand on her shoulder and she quickly grasped it with a frantic grip.

"What am I going to do, Cato?" she pleaded. "Please help me—please do something. I don't know what to do. I'm so lonely. I feel so lost and helpless. If only James would come home to live. Or if he would let me live somewhere near him. Nobody but Pastor Purdy feels sorry for me—he gives me the only comfort I get—the way I want James to do—don't make Pastor Purdy move away and leave me."

179

"All right, Aimee," he assured her, "something is going to be done about this. I don't want you to be upset about it anymore now. Go back into the house and lie down on your bed for a good long rest. You've had a lot of excitement this morning and you need to be quiet for a while. I'm going back to my office now and I'll be thinking about everything you said. I hope by this time tomorrow we can sit down and make plans that will take care of everything."

After patting her comfortingly on the shoulder, Cato picked up his briefcase and started toward his car. He had gone only a few steps when he stopped and looked back at her.

"I'm going to phone your son in Atlanta, Aimee, and ask him to come down tomorrow. This is the time for a serious family conference. Jim will want to help decide what is best to do."

"I won't listen to a word he says! He's never been a true son of mine! He's never been a true Mangrum! He left home and stayed away all this time like he's ashamed of us. He doesn't care what happens to our Mangrum homeplace. He'd rather see it burn up or torn down or anything to take it off the face of the earth. He said the Mangrums have outlived themselves in it. He said that nearly a year ago when he came here the last time and would only stay in the house for one hour and wouldn't spend the night."

"Just the same," Cato told her, "I'm going to phone Jim and ask him to be here tomorrow. Maybe he doesn't care about the Mangrum homeplace, but I know he cares about his mother."

Aimee got up and reached for the garden hoe beside the veranda steps.

"I care about the Mangrum homeplace! I'm the only Mangrum left who does! And nobody's going to tear it down and cut off all these beautiful oak trees and mimosas and drain the pond and scrape the land all bare and build houses all over it for new people who come from somewhere else and don't belong to live here. I'm going to keep strange people from living on Mangrum land who don't even care who it belonged to."

Holding the hoe with both hands, she went down the walkway to the road. She stopped there for several moments and watched the big yellow bulldozer as its grinding noise became louder and louder in her ears. With the blade of the hoe held high above her head, she crossed the drain ditch and went stumbling over the rough ground toward the bulldozer. The workman in blue coveralls, sitting on his high seat above the ground, shut off the engine when he saw Aimee coming dangerously close to the bulldozer.

When she began flailing the side of the big yellow machine with the hoe, he shouted to her to go away.

"This is my land—it's Mangrum land—it always was—it always will be—stop doing that to it!" Aimee was yelling as loudly as she could. Her hair had fallen over her face and she had to stop and brush it away in order to see what she was doing. "Go away and stop ruining it! I want it left like it is!"

"Lady," the workman said calmly, pushing the visor of his blue cloth cap above his forehead, "I don't know who you are or what your trouble is, but I'm asking you to get away from here. I was hired to do this job and I'm getting paid for it and I'm going to do it. Now, please move out of the way so I can get going again."

"I'm a Mangrum and this is Mangrum land. I don't want to have all those new houses put on it and strange people living on Mangrum land."

"Lady, I don't know what you're talking about. I don't even know why they call that Mangrum Road and I don't care. All I know is I'm hired to do what I'm doing and I'm going to keep on doing it till the job is finished."

"You talk like all the new people who move here from somewhere else. You don't belong here. Go back where you came from!"

When Cato got there, he took Aimee gently by her arm and led her away from the bulldozer. She was crying and wailing with every step she took across the field and up the walkway to the house.

Chapter 17

When Cato Boykin brought Aimee back to the house after her frenzied effort had failed to keep the big yellow bulldozer from scraping and terracing another building site, she went to bed and cried herself to sleep. Even after this long afternoon nap, she was still too despondent and disheartened to want to get out of bed, and at dusk, when finally there were no more tormenting sounds of the bulldozer, she went back to sleep for the night.

The next morning, waking up and hearing the monotonous grinding hum of the big earth-moving machine again, she still would not get up and dress. Calling Connie, she said she wanted her breakfast brought to her in bed.

Later in the morning, Aimee heard Raley Purdy leave his

room and walk down the hall with his long stride on his way to his part-time job at Gene Infinger's filling station. She wanted to call Raley to her room and have him comfort her before he left; however, not wanting him to see her in an unbecoming nightgown and with her hair uncombed, she let him go without speaking to him.

When Connie was ready to leave for the bus depot to go back to Savannah, she came to her mother's room and sat down on the side of the high, wide bed. Russ, who was going to take her downtown to the bus, carried her suitcase out of the house and went to his car in the driveway to wait while she said good-bye to Aimee.

Connie was dressed in the same stylish and expensive clothes she had worn when she had come home the previous week. After a full day and night of rest, her face was no longer as puffed and reddened as it had been when she was brought home Sunday night from the Red Carpet Motel.

When Connie leaned over and kissed her mother's cheek affectionately, Aimee reached for her hand and clutched it with a clinging grasp. Aimee's eyes blinked as they usually did when she was going to cry, but this time there were no tears.

"It's almost time for me to go, Mamma," Connie said. "Uncle Russ is waiting for me now. Is there anything you want to tell me before I leave?"

"Yes, honey." Aimee tightened the grip on her hand. "Don't go yet. Stay a little longer. There is something I want to tell you. But it's not scolding. Not a word of it. Don't think that. It's loving."

"What is it, Mamma?"

"You can be a good girl now if you want to and change your ways when you go back to Savannah, honey, and never get in trouble again like it was the other night at that motel. I'm not scolding you about that, because it's all in the past

184

now and I love you just as much as I ever did. You'll always be my precious little girl. I'm scolding myself now and I'd do anything to make up for the way I wouldn't let you go off to college years ago when you wanted to. I'm to blame for what happened after that from then on."

Connie patted her hand. "Don't worry about that, Mamma. Everything's going to be all right now."

"Well, if you'll think about something I want to tell you now, maybe it'll help make up some for it. You'll be wanting to get married before long and now's the time to start looking for the right kind of man to live with. That's a different kind of man, honey. He won't be like those other men who want a girl to sleep with only when they feel like it and not to marry. You might not think you love him much to start with, because he'll be so different, but that's the kind you learn to love and appreciate more and more all the time."

Connie smiled. "Mamma, how do you know so much about such things?"

"I was young myself once, honey, and there were a lot of men around looking for a girl to sleep with like they always do. That's why I know all about it just like every woman ought to learn for her own good as soon as she can. And the sooner you learn, the less chance there'll be of heartbreak later on. I found out that your father was the right kind of man for me to be married to and never regretted it. You're young and beautiful now and a lot of men will be begging and giving you presents and doing everything else men do to try to get you to sleep with them. Just remember that the man who really loves you enough to want to marry you will stop wanting to if you do that with a lot of other men. So find the man who adores you, honey, and he'll be faithful to you. A real adoring man won't be unfaithful if you treat him right. And then after that always stay away from all the others who only want to sleep with you and nothing else."

Connie kissed her mother's cheek again. "Mamma, you're not trying again to get me to marry Raley Purdy, are you? You know I'd never marry him. He's handsome and he's sexy, but he's so simple-minded—he can barely read and write. And that outrageous religion of his—telling people the only way they can be holy and sanctified is not to go to the bathroom on Sunday!"

"No. I'm ashamed of myself now about that. If you had wanted to marry him after what happened, I'd be happy about it, because I wanted you to marry him so you'd stay here with me and him in the same house. But all it did was make me jealous and now I wish he hadn't been in your room like that the other night. I still feel sorry for Pastor Purdy, though, and I'm going to do something for him myself."

She tightened her grip on Connie's hand.

"You're going away now, honey, and I know I won't live to see you again—"

"Mamma! Stop saying you're going to die! You promised me you'd quit talking like that. Be good now and don't say it anymore."

"I can't help it, honey. I just know I won't live much longer when everybody goes away and leaves me all alone. Even Pastor Purdy might not be satisfied to stay, either, if some other woman tempts him. But I don't want to make you promise me anything on my deathbed. And even if you don't find the right man to marry right away and keep on going to motels—"

"That's enough, Mamma," Connie told her chidingly. "You don't have to keep on talking like that."

She kissed her mother once more before drawing her hand from the tight grasp.

"I've got to hurry to the bus now. I can't stay any longer, Mamma."

"Just remember your loving mother, honey. Don't ever forget me."

Turning away from the high-posted bed with a lingering look, and wondering if she would ever see her mother alive again, Connie went from the room with tears in her eyes. As she was closing the door, Aimee smiled happily and, surprisingly, called good-bye to her in a cheerful voice without a trace of sadness. While she was going to the stairway, Connie tried to think why her mother appeared to be so glad to see her leave and she wondered if it had anything to do with her mother looking forward to being the only woman in the house with Raley Purdy.

Soon after Connie and Russ had left for the bus depot, Velma came into Aimee's furniture-cluttered room and sat down on the bed. Velma was wearing tight white shorts and a bright yellow blouse and sandals for the automobile trip to Florida. Her hanging brown hair had been drawn to the back of her neck and tied with a pale-blue bow. Her face was beaming with excitement.

"We're all packed up now and ready to leave, Mamma," she said with a nervous twisting of her fingers. "I'm so thrilled I don't know what to do. Woody and I stayed up almost all night talking about our trip and then we were awake as soon as the sun rose this morning. It's going to be our honeymoon, too—it's the first time we've been anywhere since we were married. Our car's not very good for a long trip and we don't know how far we can drive today. But we'll surely get to Florida early enough tomorrow so Woody can start practicing the numbers for the nightclub opening. I'm so excited I can hardly wait. I wish you could be there when we give the first performance. You'd be proud of Woody."

"I wouldn't be proud of him no matter what he did—except getting drafted in the army," Aimee said crossly. "Stop talking to me like that about Woody Woodruff before I say something harsh. You know what I've always thought of him for marrying into the family. All he ever does is play on that guitar of his and make up aggravating songs about me or somebody. That's nothing for you to be proud of. Now, it'll be better if you just get up now and go on off with him. You're leaving me for him and I'll never see you again. It won't be long till I'm dead, anyhow. Connie's gone and you'll be gone. Just remember me as your loving mother you left here all alone."

As when Connie had said good-bye, Aimee's round pink face was serene and untroubled. She did not cry as she usually did when she was unhappy and wanted sympathy.

"I hate to leave you, Mamma, when you talk like that. But I know you really understand. It's because I want to go. I just couldn't stay here and let Woody go without me. You were in love with Papa. You must know what this means to me. Woody and I—"

"I don't want to hear another word of that," Aimee spoke out sharply, fluttering her hands. "I've heard all I can stand. Just go on off and leave me like you want to. I'll get along the best I can somehow till the time comes for me to die."

Woody, dressed as usual in his tight black pants and with his shirttail hanging out, came from the hall where he had been waiting and sat down in one of the chairs on the far side of the room. He held his guitar on his lap and ran the comb through his hair and beard while waiting for Velma to tell her mother what he wanted to do. Aimee, smoothing the sheet over her lap, pretended not to have seen Woody come into the room.

After a long interval of silence, Velma, leaning over the bed, spoke pleadingly to her mother.

"Mamma, Woody wants to say good-bye to you in a very special kind of way. Please let him go ahead and do it. It's something he composed specially for you. You'll let him, won't you?"

188

Aimee turned her head and looked out the window as if she had not heard a word spoken.

Woody stroked the strings of the guitar several times with light touches of his fingers and then began singing the song he had composed. It was about the lasting memory of living in a great big old white mansion on Mangrum Road without having enough money to pay the rent to kindhearted Miss Mamma Aimee on Saturday night.

Aimee, with lips tightly drawn and eyes narrowed, listened to Woody until he began singing the second verse of the song. Then, glaring at him across the room, she called out in a peevish voice.

"Stop that, Woody Woodruff!" she ordered, sitting up and pointing her finger at him. "I won't allow that and I don't want to hear another word of it. It's outrageous to make up a song like that about me and sing it with the devil's own music on that guitar. All you've ever done since you've been here is think up ways to make fun of me with those aggravating songs of yours. I can hear them ringing in my ears even when you're not in the house. It was you who started calling me Miss Mamma Aimee and you even got Martha to calling me that too. I've told you I don't like being called something that sounds like a bad woman renting rooms to bad girls. You never did have any respect for me."

"But, Mamma, he's not trying to make fun of you," Velma protested. "It's Woody's way of thanking you for everything and saying good-bye. And he composed that folksong just for you. You know how he always makes up songs instead of talking very much. Let him finish singing it to you. It has a real wonderful ending—it's the best part of it. It's how he thanks you for letting us live here when we didn't have any money to live anywhere else. Won't you let him, Mamma?"

"Get out of my house, Woody Woodruff—and don't you never come back again," Aimee told him, her voice louder than ever. "I'll never know why they haven't already drafted

189

you in the army and sent you off to the other side of the world somewhere. But they'll do it yet—I've got a sure feeling in my mind about it—you just wait and see. I don't never want to see somebody like you again who marries my daughter and takes her away from me on my deathbed and makes her live in a strange part of the country so I'll never see her again."

Velma tried to kiss her mother good-bye, but Aimee pushed her away with both hands. With light touches of his fingers on the guitar strings, Woody walked out of the room playing the tune of the song he had composed and dedicated to Aimee. Velma had followed him as far as the door when Aimee called to her.

"You can come back by yourself to see me anytime you want to—if I'm still alive."

After Velma and Woody had gone, Aimee sank down into the bed, covering her face with her hands, and began sobbing for the first time that day. Suddenly the tormenting sound of the noisy bulldozer in the subdivision became so loud in her ears that she had to scream above it in order to hear her own wailing.

Chapter 18

Aimee's spasm of sobbing and wailing gradually became sub-
dued and less violent, and her eyes were closed with drowsy
weariness when she thought she heard a rapping on the door.
Slowly awakening, she raised herself from the pillow and was
sitting upright in bed when Jim Mangrum came into the room.

Aimee was not certain who he was at first. She had not seen
him for almost a year, and when she did recognize him, she
was so surprised to see him there that all she could do was
stare at him. Presently, remembering that Cato Boykin had
said he was going to ask Jim to come to see her, she wiped
her tear-dimmed eyes and saw that he was smiling at her
affectionately.

Jim was a tall, handsome man in his late thirties, with a

191

thin, dark-skinned face and straight, close-cropped black hair. He was the only Mangrum with such dark coloring and was much taller than his brother and without Graham's bulging stomach. Besides, he did not have Graham's sullen manner and quick temper and habitually quarrelsome nature. Just as there had always been since his boyhood, there was a kindly, considerate gleam in Jim's dark eyes, and he had a way of listening attentively when anyone was speaking to him as if nothing else in the world was of any importance at the time.

Jim was still smiling when he crossed the room and sat down on the chair beside the bed.

"Hello, Mamma," he said.

"James, I didn't know who you were—I was half asleep—I wasn't expecting you—I thought it might be somebody else who looks a lot like you."

He reached out and put his hand on her arm.

"What are you doing here, James?"

There was a suspicious narrowing of her eyes.

"I came to see you, Mamma."

"Why did you do that?"

"Well, don't you think it's time for me to come to see my own mother again? It'll soon be a whole year since I was here the last time."

"Are you going to stay and spend the night?"

He shook his head. "Mamma, you always ask the same thing every time, don't you?"

"Why won't you, James?" she pleaded.

"You know me by now. And if you could see some of the patients in my office from morning to night waiting for treatment, you wouldn't want me to stay here and neglect them."

"Well, what is the really truthful reason you came here now and surprised me like this?"

192

"Mamma," he said, his manner serious and intent, "I want to talk to you about several things—important things."

"What important things?" she asked suspiciously.

"You and Graham."

"Who sent for you? It was Cato Boykin, wasn't it?"

Jim nodded. "Yes, he did."

"That busybody! He's always butting in and trying to run my life for me!"

"Mamma, whatever you think about it, I'm glad Mr. Boykin didn't wait another day to phone me. It was bad enough for you to keep on selling off the land and spending the money to support all the people in this house the way you've been doing, but now you've taken in a fly-by-night itinerant evangelist who's no kin to us and you're giving him free room and board. The next thing would be to sell more land and give him the money. Mr. Boykin told me that you had agreed to let him sell the house and all remaining land so a trust could be established for your protection before the property dwindled away until nothing was left for you. As I understand it, you told him he could sell everything and then yesterday you changed your mind and—"

"Cato Boykin's got no right to go behind my back and phone you about that. He's a meddlesome old busybody. I can get along without Cato Boykin or anybody telling me what to do. If I want to change my mind, nobody can stop me. I feel sorry for everybody in my house—and that includes Pastor Purdy, too. I hated some of them while I was feeling sorry for them—Katie Snoddyhouse and Woody Woodruff—but I had to put up with them as long as I did because I was trying to keep Velma and Russell from leaving me. That's why it's none of Cato Boykin's business trying to stop me from what I do."

"All right, Mamma, we'll leave him out of it. We'll say it's none of his business. But it's our business. Yours and mine.

193

And it's serious business, too. I haven't interfered before, and purposely stayed out of it, because it made you happy being a do-gooder and amateur philanthropist. But you went too far when you started supporting that evangelist."

"I don't want Pastor Purdy criticized. I took a special interest in him because—well, just because."

"Because what? What is the reason?"

There was an accusing sharpness in the tone of her voice when she answered after a moment's hesitation.

"You left home and wouldn't come back—and wouldn't let me live anywhere near you."

He nodded encouragingly, wanting her to keep on talking.

"James, I missed you and I was so lonely. I just had to take care of somebody in your place. Because you weren't here like I wanted you to be. And Pastor Purdy came along and reminded me so much of you. If you saw him, you'd see how much he looks like you."

"I'm sorry, Mamma. I didn't realize I was making you that unhappy. I've been so busy with my practice and taking care of my family that I failed to consider you enough. But we're going to do something about that right away."

Aimee smiled for the first time and a glow of happiness began spreading over her round pink face.

"What do you want me to do, James?" she asked, watching him expectantly.

"Mamma, now listen to me. This's the way it's going to be from now on. I'm going to get you a fine apartment close to me in Atlanta and arrange for Graham to live where he'll be much better off than where he is now. This property is going to be sold—the house and all—and the money put into a trust for you the way Papa wanted it done. I'm not going to let you keep on living the way you've been doing. That's why I'm not going to let you stay here with Graham any longer. Mr. Boykin told me that Graham has been in several fights lately

194

and that's not a good sign. He'll have to be taken care of somewhere else. It's too dangerous the way it is now."

Instead of protesting, Aimee was smiling contentedly.

"Now, Mamma, I asked Dr. Price to meet me at the airport this morning and he's downstairs now waiting to see you. I want you to talk to him and listen to him. You've known Dr. Price for many years and you have confidence in him. Please cooperate with him."

"If he's going to talk about sending Graham away, he can save himself the trouble. I'm all ready to go live near you, but I want Graham to go, too. I'm not going to let anybody send Graham away somewhere else. Nobody will take care of him like I do."

"Dr. Price will talk to you about Graham and anything else you wish. The important thing is for you to be reasonable and cooperate. Just remember that I want you to listen very carefully to whatever he says. Will you do that for me, Mamma?"

"Well, I'll listen to him and he can talk all he wants to. But I'm not going to sell off the last of the Mangrum property so they can build new houses on it for strange people to live in. That's why I've stopped trusting Cato Boykin. He keeps on trying to get me to sell everything so he can get rich off of me and let strange people build houses on our land. But he can't trick me, and I won't let Dr. Price trick me, neither. I'm going to protect the Mangrum property as long as I live and keep Graham with me, too."

"Mamma, you've got to be more reasonable than that," Jim said patiently. "It's no way for you to talk before you hear what Dr. Price is going to say. You're a big girl and not a little child. Now, be good and behave yourself. If you talk like that to Dr. Price, he won't stand for it. He'll give you doctor's orders and make you behave."

Smiling appealingly as if she had been chastised like a small girl who had misbehaved and wanted to be forgiven and lovingly hugged, Aimee moved closer to Jim.

"All right, James. I'll behave. I'll listen to Dr. Price. But I don't want you in the room while he's here. I'm not going to let my own son be a doctor to me. That would be indecent."

"You're absolutely right about that, Mamma. We're in complete agreement."

Jim stood up and put his hand on his mother's shoulder.

"You are an ideal patient, Mamma. I wish all my other patients were as cooperative as you are. Now, I'm going downstairs and ask Dr. Price to come up. I'll see you again after you and he have a good talk."

"Don't you dare come back in here till I'm ready for you, James. I won't allow such an indecent thing."

"Don't worry. I won't."

He walked away from the bed.

"James!" she called urgently as he was leaving the room. "How are my precious grandchildren? It's been two years since you and your wife brought them to see me. I miss them so much! Do they still remember me? Do they know who I am—have they forgotten their grandmother?"

"All three are well and happy, Mamma, and they talk about you and ask how soon it'll be before you come to live near them. That's how much they remember you."

Once more, Aimee called to him as he was about to leave the room.

"James! Wait! Before you go, hand me my mirror and the comb and brush on the table over there. I don't want Dr. Price to see me looking awful."

Jim took the things to his mother and then went downstairs to Dr. Price and Cato Boykin, who were waiting on the veranda. He nodded to Dr. Price as he motioned toward his mother's bedroom. Dr. Price left without a word.

When Dr. Price knocked lightly on the door and then

196

walked into her room, Aimee had just finished hastily fluffing her graying hair and powdering her face. She was sitting upright in bed as she waited for him, a pleasant expression on her round pink face.

Dr. Price, a kindly-appearing man in his sixties, was of medium height and comfortably overweight. Even though his bushy eyebrows were still black, he had thinning white hair and a graying moustache that drooped slightly over the corners of his mouth. His square-jawed face was rosy in color and he might have been mistaken for a well-to-do retired barber or bartender instead of an active family physician who took pride in making house calls to his patients. In addition to being highly respected by the younger doctors for his medical knowledge and ability, he was also widely known and easily recognizable on the street because of his unusual appearance. Seemingly unmindful of heat or cold, Dr. Price wore a vest with his dark-gray suits in summer and winter alike, but never an overcoat in the coldest weather. Moreover, nobody could recall ever having seen him when he was not wearing a white-on-blue polka-dot bow tie and carrying a leather-cased thermometer and several cigars protruding from the upper pocket of his jacket. One of his jocular remarks, when a matter of divorce was mentioned, was that he was unqualified to offer advice because he had been married to the same woman for thirty-seven years and had not had the opportunity to find out by experience if a different wife would iron his shirts any better.

"Well, Mrs. Mangrum," Dr. Price addressed her with a modest wink as he sat down in the chair beside the bed and put his black leather satchel on the floor, "it was very pleasing to me—"

"Why do you always call me that, Dr. Price? You act like you don't want to get to know me personally. Why don't you call me Aimee?"

"Mrs. Mangrum," he said with a stern look, "I've found by experience that my patients are ideally cooperative and react much better to treatment when the relationship remains impersonal. I suppose it could be said that I belong to the old school. But, be that as it may, it's been my experience that it's the best way to influence my patients to take the full medication I prescribe and not throw some of the pills down the toilet bowl. There's nothing better for a patient's welfare than scaring the wits out of him—he'll take his full medication if he's afraid he might die if he doesn't. Now, as I was saying just now when I came in, it was very pleasing to me to have those two gentlemen downstairs arrange for me to have the pleasure of calling on you today. You've been exceedingly healthy and had no need of me for I don't know how long. As it is, it's been many months since I've had the opportunity to be in your company. But I hadn't forgotten what a charming lady you are, Mrs. Mangrum."

"Now, you stop that, Dr. Price," Aimee said, briefly covering her face with both hands. "It won't do any good to try to flatter me like that so you can get me to do what you want. I know your ways. You don't fool me for one minute. I'm not a silly young girl who'd believe every word a man says."

"Of course you're not, Mrs. Mangrum. You are a sophisticated lady and much too wise and knowing about life to let yourself be victimized by predatory men. Only a fool would think you could be led into his nefarious clutches."

"Is that what you really think of me, Dr. Price?"

"Yes. And you remind me of another enchanting lady I once knew. Like you, she had beauty and intelligence and an ingratiating personality in her favor. A remarkable woman. But, unlike you, unfortunately, she was lacking the one essential female characteristic that prevented her from achieving complete fulfillment and personal happiness. A very sad case."

"What happened to her, Dr. Price?"

"That's the sad part. I tried to give her guidance, but she resented my suggestions and continued on her heedless way. I've lost track of her now. She disappeared, probably thinking she could run away from her unhappiness. I often wonder if she ever came to realize the mistake she was making and rectified it, or if she's living out her unfortunate existence never knowing the ultimate contentment and happiness she could have had with that one essential female characteristic. A very sad case."

"Dr. Price, what was that essential female thing she didn't have?" Aimee asked at once.

He took some papers and envelopes from his pocket and began searching through them one by one as if deeply concerned about something of importance that may have been lost. After a while, gravely shaking his head, he put the bundle back into his coat pocket.

Aimee was gripping her fingers and breathing more rapidly all the time. There was increasing tension in her expression as she waited to hear what he would say. Dr. Price opened his medical satchel and began looking through it for the missing paper.

She could stand the suspense no longer.

"Dr. Price! I've got to know! What was that—the thing you said about that woman!"

"Oh, that?" he said as if surprised that she would still be interested in what he had said about a former patient.

"Yes! Tell me—I've got to know!"

"Well, Mrs. Mangrum, there's a medical term for it, but let's just say that she was addicted to the practice of wearing a man's britches under her skirt. Figuratively speaking, of course. Such a sad case."

"What does that mean?"

"Instead of glorifying her natural gift of womanhood, which of course means being feminine and receptive, she set out—

perversely—to dominate and ravish everybody in her realm without being equipped by nature with the necessary male appendages for the function. And so, her inability to be both male and female resulted in acute frustration and neurosis. In other words, she became an obnoxious bitch. Such a very sad case."

Dr. Price closed his satchel and stood up. After counting Aimee's pulse, he put his hand on her forehead for a few moments.

"Am I all right, Dr. Price?" she asked meekly. "Is anything wrong with me?"

"Not a thing in the world, Mrs. Mangrum. You are in splendid condition. I wish all my ailing patients had your physical and mental good health."

"You didn't put your thermometer in my mouth."

"There's no need for that."

"Are you going to give me some pills to take?"

"No, Mrs. Mangrum. You are not in need of medication. Pills are for the ill."

"But don't I need tranquilizing? You gave me that the last time you came to see me."

"There's no need for that this time. You are normal and rational now."

"One time you gave me an injection right here behind that made me feel awfully good. Won't you even do that now?"

Shaking his head, he picked up his black leather satchel and was leaving the room when Aimee called to him anxiously.

"Dr. Price—I thought you'd say something else to me before you left. Didn't you forget? James said you'd talk about—about Graham—"

"That's not necessary, Mrs. Mangrum. You are an intelligent woman with keen perception and a mother's instinct to want to do what is best for her son's welfare. You've been exceedingly cooperative the whole time I've been here. I'm confident now that you'll have a reasonable attitude about any suggestion Jim offers and will want to do what is best for Graham. Good-bye, Mrs. Mangrum."

Chapter 19

In the late afternoon, after Dr. Price and Cato Boykin had driven Jim Mangrum to the airport so he could take the plane back to Atlanta, Graham brought a plate of cold potatoes and ham to his mother and then went downstairs to eat his own supper alone in the dining room. Russ, taking his shaving kit and a clean shirt with him for the first time, had already left the house for Telfair Street to spend the night.

During the afternoon there had been a brief but violent thunderstorm that had left deep puddles of water in the driveway. The soaking rain had made the ground too muddy for the big yellow bulldozer to do any more earth-moving in the subdivision until the next day, and there was a peaceful silence for the first time since early morning.

It was the beginning of what would be nearly an hour of late spring twilight when Aimee finished her supper and lay quietly in bed, thinking about Jim's forceful and authoritative manner of telling her what his plans were for her and Graham.

For the first time in many years, calm and content with no anxiety on her mind now that Jim had ruled what was to be done, she felt at peace with the world and everybody in it. (*Aimee had worked herself into a dangerous state of mind over the years and finally she was on the verge of a complete emotional and mental collapse. She had become obsessed with the idea that Jim was purposely neglecting and rejecting her, which he was not conscious of, and resentment and retaliation were driving her blindly to irrational attitudes. And of course Graham's unfortunate condition contributed to her unhappiness. She made a pretense of being compassionate toward him, but all the time she secretly hated him and blamed him for Jim's neglect of her. I may be wrong, but it seems to me that that was the reason she encouraged Graham to get into fights—she wanted something fatal to happen to Graham so Jim would come home or let her live with him. All this resulted in extremes of mother love and mother hate. It's not easy to simplify such a complex matter, but perhaps this is a partial explanation of Aimee's attitudes and actions.*) Now that she was going to Atlanta to live close to Jim, and confident that she could eventually persuade Jim to let her move into his home, Aimee had no desire to stay at the Mangrum homeplace any longer or to keep Raley Purdy with her. She knew she had befriended Raley only because she wanted somebody to take Jim's place in her life, and Raley resembled Jim so closely that it gave her the feeling of being with him. And now that she no longer needed Raley, she wondered how soon she could send him on his way.

There had been so much excitement while Jim and Dr.

Price had been there during the day that she had not been able to take her usual afternoon nap, and she was beginning to feel pleasantly drowsy when she heard Raley Purdy's long strides in the hall.

After a few moments, she slowly opened her eyes and there he stood in the doorway.

"I'm so glad to see you, Pastor Purdy," she called to him. "I've been thinking about you. Come on in. I want you to hold my hand while I tell you all about everything that happened today. I don't know when I've felt so peaceful and happy before. I want you to know all about it."

Raley started to come into the room, but suddenly Aimee held up both hands and hid her face.

"But not right now," she told him, still hiding her face. "I want to fix myself up first—I'm an awful sight for anybody to see me now like I am. You go to your room and just wait a little while. Then come back and hold my hand. It won't be long."

As soon as he had gone, Aimee got up and put on her best nightgown and spent a long time fluffing her graying hair and powdering herself. She went back to bed after looking appraisingly at herself in the mirror and carefully adjusting the thin pink nightgown over her breasts and around her neck just as she wanted it.

Sitting upright in bed with the pillows behind her back and the hem of the sheet folded neatly over her lap, she waited no longer to call Raley. When she heard him leaving his room, she placed her hand on the edge of the bed for him.

Smiling shyly, Raley came into the room with the big box of candy in its green wrapping and red bow. He placed it on her lap with an awkward twist of his body and then sat down in the chair beside the bed.

"What in the world, Pastor Purdy!" she exclaimed.

"It's for you, Mrs. Mangrum. It's a present."

204

"I didn't expect anything like this."

"You can have it if you want to."

"A present—for me!"

She stroked the green wrapping with delicate touches.

"I could almost cry, Pastor Purdy—getting a present from you. It makes me feel so warm and shivery all over at the same time. You're so thoughtful of me. But you shouldn't spend your money on me like this. You're treating me like a young girl—the same way you did Connie and Velma. I hardly know what to say."

"Well, it's just what I wanted to do."

"And I'm so pleased and surprised—you're so kind and thoughtful—it'd be a shame for anybody to treat you mean." Aimee leaned toward him and touched him with her hand. "Come closer. You're so far away. Sit right here next to me on the bed. I want you close to me so I can touch you better. It's all right. Don't be afraid. I still feel sorry for you—I still want to do something for you. And there won't be another time after this—after today it'll be too late—my wonderful son James—"

Raley sat down beside her and she took his hand and kissed it again and again.

"You do want me to do something for you, don't you?" she said, bringing his hand to her breast. "I didn't give you the land for your church like I promised and now it's too late. They won't let me give it away now. But I still want to do something for you. And you want me to, don't you?"

His face brightened with expectation.

"Then you don't have to wait any longer," she told him, pulling him closer. "Come on. You can get under the sheet with me right now. It's what I want you to do. Don't be shy about it. Just act the way you feel like doing."

Lifting the sheet, she moved to the middle of the bed.

"Mrs. Mangrum—"

Aimee suddenly dropped the sheet and tucked it securely around her.

Graham had come into the room without knocking on the door and he was standing at the foot of the bed. With a gasp of annoyance, Aimee pushed Raley away and jerked the sheet completely over herself until only her face was uncovered. Raley, looking around and seeing Graham, hastily moved to the chair beside the bed.

"What do you want, Graham?" she spoke to him severely, wondering how long he had been there listening and watching them on the bed. "What are you doing here, Graham?"

"I came to take the dishes downstairs."

"Well, there they are on the table. You can take them and go away now."

Graham did not move from the foot of the bed.

"Why don't you go on and do that, Graham?"

"What's in that box?"

"A present."

"Who gave it to you?"

"Pastor Purdy. And it's candy. I'll give you some after a while when I open it up. You just go on downstairs now and wait. I'll let you know when you can have some."

"What's he giving you candy for?"

"It's just like any present, Graham. People like to do things like that. He wanted to do something nice for me."

"I don't want to let him give you presents. I know why he did it. He wants to be in here like he was in Connie's room—and he tried to get in Velma's room—to give them presents, too. I've seen that box in his room where he hides things under his bed."

"But it's all right, Graham," she said soothingly, trying to keep him from being upset. "It won't do any harm for him to give me a present. I'll call you after a while and give you some of the candy. I'll save a lot for you."

"Why can't I have some now?"

"Because I want to look at the pretty wrapping around it some more first. Now, you be good so I'll like you, Graham. Go on downstairs with the dishes. You want me to like you, don't you?"

Nodding reluctantly and with a sullen look first at his mother and then at Raley, but saying nothing more, Graham picked up the dishes and left the room.

They both listened to the sound of Graham's stomping footsteps as he went down the stairway to the kitchen.

"It'll be better to wait a little while now, Pastor Purdy," Aimee said presently, drawing the sheet tightly under her chin. "I'm so nervous now—Graham might come back—and I'm afraid he'd knock the door down if we locked it. There'll be plenty of time later. You just wait. I won't forget."

Raley listened intently for a long time as if fearful that Graham would come back upstairs at any moment.

"Mrs. Mangrum," Raley said presently in an uneasy voice, "I think I'd better leave—"

"Please don't go away now," she begged, grasping his arm. "Don't leave me now. There's so much I want to tell you. And this's the best time to do it."

There was an unusually loud squeak of a door somewhere nearby and then after that there was silence once more.

"Before anything else, Pastor Purdy," she said, watching the doorway, "I want you to know how sorry I am that I didn't do nothing at all to help you get your church going. You know I started out to do that because I felt sorry for you and wanted to do something for you, but the wisdom of fate makes everything different now. My son James is going to take care of me and be in charge of everything from now on. I feel like a different woman now to have a wonderful son like James taking care of me and telling me what to do. That's why I promised him I wouldn't change my mind about anything from now on. He's going to take me to Atlanta to live close to him and my grandchildren and find a nice home somewhere for Graham. But I don't want you to go away and have hard feelings about me for not keeping my promise to help you some for your church—that's why I want to do something else for you now to make up for it."

Raley, looking appealing at Aimee, moved to the edge of his chair.

"Ain't you going to give no money before you leave?"

"No, Pastor Purdy, I won't have any to give you now. My son James—"

"That's a mean way to treat me. All this time I thought I'd get a lot of money this way."

"You can look for a kind-hearted woman somewhere around town to help you like that. Just go around to houses and knock on doors like you did here the first time. Somebody will feel sorry for you like I did at the start and give you something. There're a lot of women like me who'll do that."

He covered his face with his hands as if either praying or in deep thought. Finally, when he looked at Aimee again, much of his anger and disappointment had vanished.

"When are you going to move away, Mrs. Mangrum?"

"I'm going to start packing up tomorrow."

"And I can't stay here in the house no more?"

"No. But I'm sorry about it."

Raley looked down at his hands and slowly counted his fingers one by one.

"The rent's just about all used up at the place I rented for my church and to live in upstairs. And I've got so far behind trying to get it going that it'd be too hard now to get it running again. Besides, it don't look like I can get enough people in Augusta to pay enough money in the collection to make it worthwhile. I figure I'd be better off if I went to Savannah and started all over again. From what I heard said about it when Connie was here, Savannah is a real sinful place and Billy Graham would want me to go where the most sin is. If you'd let me know how to find her down there, maybe she'd help me get located."

As she listened to Raley, Aimee was the first to see Graham coming through the doorway. With a shriek of terror, she put her hands to her face. Raley, startled by her sudden outcry, turned around to see what had frightened her.

Graham was pointing a large rusty revolver directly at his mother as he came closer to the bed.

"Don't—Graham—don't," Aimee pleaded frantically. "I won't like you if you don't stop pointing that pistol at me! You want me to like you, don't you? Graham! Stop that and say something!"

He was at the foot of the bed then.

"You don't like me. You tell me lies about liking me. You're going to let them send me away somewhere. You want them to do that. I heard them talking. You're going to let them lock me up where I can't get out. You don't like me no more at all. You like that preacher better than me. I'm mad at you."

"Don't say that, Graham! I do like—"

Without another word, he fired the pistol at his mother until there were no more bullets left. Aimee sank slowly into the bed with only a feeble murmur.

Raley jumped to his feet and moved backward to the wall as quickly as he could.

Graham had turned and was facing Raley.

"Graham—what you going to do now—"

"Hand me that box of candy," Graham ordered.

Raley was quick to do as he had been told.

"Now, I'll shoot you," Graham told him.

"But I'm a preacher! Don't shoot a preacher!"

Graham laughed at him.

"And that's my own pistol—you found it under my bed—my

daddy gave it to me to protect myself! Don't shoot me with my own pistol!"

Holding the box of candy with one hand, Graham pointed the revolver at Raley and pressed the trigger time after time with a harmless clicking.

"It's all used up," he said, smiling a little. "It won't shoot no more."

Graham put the pistol into his pocket and began to tear the green wrapping from the box. When he threw the wrapping aside and saw the chocolate candy, he stuffed one of the pieces into his mouth and chewed it greedily. After eating a second piece, and carefully holding the box in both hands so none of the candy would fall out, he left the room and slowly stomped down the hall.

About the Author

From the day of his birth in Coweta County, Georgia,
until he reached the age of twenty, Erskine Caldwell
rarely lived longer than a year in one place. The son
of a Presbyterian minister, he left home at fourteen to wander
through the Deep South, Mexico, and Central America.
When he was seventeen, he enrolled at Erskine College,
Due West, S.C., but remained only a short time. His next
attempt to complete his education was when he entered
the University of Virginia on a scholarship, and there
he began writing short stories. Later he attended the
University of Pennsylvania, and then spent eight years
in Maine, where he wrote *Tobacco Road* and *God's Little Acre*.
The latter, which the *Saturday Review* called "one of
the finest studies of Southern poor whites that has ever
come into our literature," is probably the most widely
read contemporary American novel. During these years,
he worked as a seaman, cotton picker, cabdriver, bodyguard,
cub reporter, cook, and waiter.

Best known for his novels and short stories, Mr. Caldwell
is also a journalist of note, having been a newspaper and
radio correspondent in Europe during World War II.
Once married to the *Life* photographer Margaret
Bourke-White, Mr. Caldwell now lives near San Francisco
with his present wife, Virginia. They spend a good deal
of time traveling, both in the United States and abroad.
His most recent books include *In Search of Bisco*,
The Last Night of Summer, and *Close to Home*.